I0679203

LOYALTY is
A FAULT

A NOVEL BY TYEMEASE

CHAPTER 1

"Chad didn't want to come. I guess he think y'all might try to do something to him, because he don't have all that money yet. I told him since you was one of ma brothers that I'll talk to you about giving him some more time to pay you."

"He fucking up. It ain't me he gotta worry about. The Sheik growing impatient. When he gets upset the dark skies open up and he come down on dudes. A hundred stacks ain't no chump change," Raheem said.

"I know I know. Alright, how about I pay his debt? I'll bring an extra ten thousand in every time I re-up."

"You'll do that for him?"

"Yeah," Kenyan said.

"That must really be ya man."

"Yeah, I don't wonna see him get killed."

"What if something happens and you can't pay?"

"Then y'all do whatever y'all was going to do to him. Nothing is going to happen though. I'm going to make sure of that."

"Alright, I'm not making any promises, but I'ma talk to the Sheik, then I'll let you know. Until then I advise him not to show his face around."

"That's not going to be a problem. I'll let him know," Kenyan said with confidence because his manz Chad was already laying low, afraid for his life. He knew that the people he owed money to didn't play.

Kenyan left the house with his bags in hand. He looked up and down the block for safety measures, that was out of habit. As he looked to the left down the street, he saw a big bald headed dude with a big beard. He wore a long coat. Kenyan could only imagine how big the gun was underneath it. There was also a few other guys on porches of houses, acting regular, but they all had the same purpose, which was to dead anybody who tried anything stupid.

"Here, hold this," Kenyan said getting in the car and putting the bag on Terron's lap.

Terron didn't have to look in it to know what it was. It was only one reason they were there. He knew if by any chance that they were to get pulled over by the cops, that it was on him to run like hell with that bag.

"The shit I do for dudes. I can't believe it sometimes," Kenyan said shaking his head. "Light that Dutch up," he said while pulling off.

Terron put the bag on the floor, lit the Dutch, then passed it too Kenyan. He grabbed the Dutch with his right hand and kept his left hand at twelve O'clock on the steering wheel as they rode through the streets of Camden in his rimmed up Yukon Denali truck. The sun was reflecting off of the diamonds in his Rolex. Clear smoke filled the truck making it seem like they were literally on cloud nine.

Terron looked up to his manz Kenyan. Even though at the age of twenty three, Kenyan only had five years on him. For many reasons he looked up to him.

One of the major ones was that he played on a different level than the average dude, especially dudes his age. He got money and was connected. To Terron, that's what it was about. Star status in the hood. With no brothers or father figure in his life growing up, Kenyan became both to Terron without even knowing it.

"What happened back there," Terron asked?

"I just saved Chad's life, that's what just happened. He owed the brothers a hundred thousand. You know them dudes don't play. They mess around and would've taken his head off, literally! I'm saying, I talked to them and told them that I'll make sure they get their money."

"That's some real shit, not just anybody would've done that."

"You right, that's my manz though. When it comes to ya manz, it's not supposed to be nothing you wouldn't do to get them out of a jam. Always be there for ya dudes. Remember that, it's principles to this thing. It's a lot of unwritten rules that dudes are supposed to be holding up. It's not like dudes don't know them, they're just weak. The weak are the majority, so the ones who were acting strong are actually folding to the weak shit because that was never them, but the real dudes are going to remain strong no matter what. Time reveals everything."

Terron was sitting there listening to the words of wisdom from his manz. He was taking heed to everything. One could say that he was a student of the game because all he did was sit back, observe and soak up all he could. He implemented nothing but the real and the thorough. He hated the fake and the weak.

****

"You good, I told them that I'll pay the debt."

"Word! Good looking bro, but how you going to do that?"

"I got that, don't worry about it. Just let me get the money that you do have."

Chad became hesitant when Kenyan asked for his money. "For what," he asked?

"So it can add on to what I have to give them. What you think you don't have to come off of nothing? It don't work like that."

"I'm saying, I ain't got much."

"We'll, give me what you got."

"Then what am I going to have?"

"You going to have ya life. You can always make more money. You lucky I'm not making you sell that car."

Chad knew that Kenyan had a valid point, he went upstairs and came back down with the money. Kenyan looked at what he had and just from a glance he could tell that it was far off. Kenyan counted the money. When he was finished, he looked at Chad in disgust.

"That's all you working with is thirty thousand? You out here fronting, wearing Gucci, riding around in ya

BMW, running through these chicks like everything sweet, like you up a mill."

Terron was looking at Kenyan tell Chad about himself. His respect for Chad was diminishing by the second. Thirty thousand was a lot to Terron but because of the way Chad moved, Terron assumed that he was sitting at least on a million. Now that Terron was as close as he was to Kenyan, he was seeing things for what they really were.

Chad, Kenyan and Kenyan's brother Kenny sold drugs in the circle out Whiteboy Fairview. Terron started out as a trapper but after seeing how committed and loyal he was Kenyan decided to give him a position and keep him close.

****

Raheem walked in with a duffle bag weighing one side of his shoulder down. He dropped it to the ground relieving himself. He unzipped it revealing the money that was neatly stacked on top of each other. The money was the earnings from all the weight sells he made for Anwar's drug operation. Raheem was his main runner.

"Chad couldn't pay his bill Sheik." (Sheik is an Arabic word used meaning elder, Trible leader, or old man. All of these applied to Anwar) "I don't know what's going on with him, I haven't seen him. His manz Kenyan said that he was going to pay everything. He just asking for him to be spared. He gave me Ten thousand on top of the three bricks he bought. He said, every time he re-up that he would at least come with an extra ten. I told him that I'll check with you to see if it was alright."

Anwar sat at his desk with his reading glasses on. A chew stick was hanging out of his mouth while he looked at the newspaper. While Raheem was talking, Anwar never took his eyes off of the paper.

Anwar was a true old head with a family and businesses. He been in the game for decades and made tens of millions. He was well connected, not only with drug connections but with politicians and authority figures, state and county wide.

Raheem stood there waiting for Anwar to respond when he slowly put the papers down, took his glasses off and said, "Who you talking about the brown skin slim brother?"

"That's him, the one him and his brother look like twins."

"I'll allow it on the strength of him. You can tell the boys to fall back."

He was referring to the hit that was out on Chad. Even though Anwar wasn't around the hood or the stuff that be going on, he had his ways of finding out what was going on and who was who. He was well invested in the streets. He knew who Kenyan was from seeing him in Jumu'ah (Islamic religious services) on Friday's. Kenyan knew that Anwar ran security at the Mosque, but that was it. He had no idea that the coke he was buying came from him or that he was one of the biggest drug dealers in Camden.

CHAPTER 2

6:15am on a Friday morning Terron woke up yawning. He stretched, got up, took a piss, then washed his hands and face. After doing so he iced grilled himself in a little 5 by 8 plastic mirror that was held up by a magnet and stuck to another messed up mirror with a metal trim. Every day since being locked up he been waking up on the wrong side of the bed, angry that he was in the situation he was in, with the kind of time he had. Six years ago, Friday would have been a day that him and his manz would of went out and did their thing at a club or something, but now he stood in a 6 by 12 sell in East Jersey State Prison with forty five years to life getting ready to go to the mess hall.

The C.O. popped the gates, he bent his head down to get out of his sell and onto the narrow tier. He stood on the tier and looked in his sell thinking how people probably had bigger dog houses then this. All the outside gates were made out of metal bars while the dividing walls were made from a slab of metal. On days like the present one, when it was baking hot outside, the three fans he had wasn't doing much of anything because there was no central air.

Terron walked a few sells down to this FOI old head he always built with. The shelves on old head walls were filled with books. Terron didn't know his story or too much about him. That's not what they talked about.

He was always giving Terron a book that would be the topic of their discussions.

"What's up Black Man, What's the word for the day?"

Old head was shaving his bald head like he did every morning. He didn't go to the mess hall. He always had the kitchen workers bring him food.

"The word for the day is loyalty."

"What about it," Terron asked wanting to know why he chose that word?

"Loyalty is overrated. Go meditate on that and we'll build on it at a later date."

Terron nodded his head in agreement. The whole time he was repeating the phase over and over in his mind. The C.O. opened the main gate and Terron went to mess. As he walked through the tie two there was about twelve C.O.'s. He could feel the tension between the inmates and the C.O.'s. The tie two was where the C.O.'s randomly pulled guys over for quick pat downs for any drugs or shanks during whatever moments were being called out. It was always Terron's thing to walk through there with his head up, chest out, and his poker face on. He knew the C.O.'s was always trying to figure dudes out. Amongst them was always a dickhead or two that felt like they were state troopers, who was miserable at home, either racist or one of them black C.O.'s who was trying to prove himself to the white man. Terron had ended up getting pulled over by a woman. He was always willing to let them get their feel on. She was caressing him more than searching for anything. Terron walked in the mess hall of a few hundred dudes. In there everybody sat with dudes that dealt with what they dealt with. The Christians, the Muslims, the Bloods, the Crips, the neutrals, even the white boys had their own section. Terron got his food and went over to the Muslim section and sat with his brothers.

"As salammu aliakum," he said greeting the table.

"Wa alaykum salam," They responded.

Terron was talking to his brother when they heard a loud noise. The first thing they did was look around to see where it was going down at. It was another dude from Camden fighting a white boy that owed him some money and cigarettes over some bets they had made on some football games. Kas was brutally smashing dude out. He was a big boy. The white boy didn't have a chance. It was two gated up towers in the mess hall, with two to three C.O.'s in each of them. The sergeant was yelling over the blow horn for them to stop. The code was called and about twenty more C.O.'s showed up, but they stood on the outside of the gates. They never came in the mess hall.

Kas blacked out on dude. Slamming him on his head, stumping him out, jumping off of the table on him. Terron seen dude eyes go behind his head a few times. He knew Kas, they were cool, but they didn't really have a friendship like that for him to be getting in his business. The dudes he really did deal with like that was just sitting there watching him smash dude out. After he knocked dude out, he put him in a wrestling move called the Boston Crab. He sat on his back facing his legs and put both of legs under his arms then leaned all the way back to dude's head. The mess hall was silent as everyone heard a big crack and pop as Kas broke dude back.

"Dam," Terron said to himself. Only the people closest to him heard him. He heard someone start to cry. He turned towards the gate to see that it was a black lady C.O..

"Stop him, please. He going to kill him," she pleaded from the other side of the gate.

Nobody did anything though. Kas drugged the guy over to the coffee machine, put him under it, then turned it on. By now dude was dead, when the coffee hit him, he didn't move even though the coffee was scolding hot. It immediately started melting the skin off of his face. Everyone looked away, cringing from the gruesome site. One of the C.O.'s was crying like crazy now. The medical unit was waiting outside of the gate to provide medical care, but they couldn't do anything until they brought the guy to the gate. Kas sat on top of the table like King Kong as he watched the coffee melt dude away. Somebody tried to remove dude from under the coffee, but Kas said something that scared dude away.

It was hours before Terron got back to his cell. That whole night he couldn't stop thinking about how Kas did dude dirty. He did some dirt in his life but nothing like what he saw that day. Kas rip dude apart like he was a lion in the jungle. That was the first time Terron really realized how serious prison was. That incident showed him that not everyone was going to make it home alive.

Just the thought that it was a possibility that he could die in prison made him reflect on his situation. He was still fresh down on a 45 to life sentence. His hopes were high on giving time back, but so was everybody's. Hope is what kept guys going in his situation. He still had money for his lawyer and the lawyers were saying that he had good grounds. Terron laid on his bonk in reverie, thinking about his appeal and his past.

CHAPTER 3

"Bro, once I pay these guys the money this dude owe, I'm a look out for you. You could start buying weight, or I'll front you. Whatever you want to do, alright?"

"I'm with that," Terron responded to Kenyan. Him being able to buy weight meant more money for him. Running the block was money, but buying weight was next level so he was looking forward to it.

"Right now, we in grind mode. No clubbing, none of that shit. Stack everything," Kenyan said.

"I heard."

"I'm telling you don't ever get in debt with the connect or anybody. Dudes be having their priorities messed up, trying to ball out when they know they don't have it like that. You have to get ya money up before you start to shine. When I say up, I don't mean twenty thousand. That's Childs play, I'm talking real money. In the process you making sure the connect get his, straight paper. That way you always have it. You never want to burn bridges with the connect because there might come a time when you messed up. That's when ya credit come into play. Everybody takes losses in this game, it's how you bounce back.

"You good Chad," Kenyan asked as they walked in the upstairs room?

Chad was sitting at a little table bagging up coke. Since Kenyan took on his debt, he made him the bag up boy until his debt was paid off. Off course Chad felt like Kenyan was trying to play him but he also knew the reality was if he showed his face and that debt wasn't paid then he could get killed.

"Yeah, I'm good. Just tired."

"How much is this," Kenyan asked referring to what was already bagged up?

"That's twenty G packs," Chad answered.

Kenyan picked them up and gave them to Terron. Terron put them into a plastic bag then tucked it into his coat.

"This shit tiresome bro, I don't know if I can keep doing this. Ma fingertips burned." He showed Kenyan his burned fingers from sealing baggies. There was coke ingrained in his fingertips. He had a hot iron plugged in that he would seal the baggies with. Once he tapped the baggies on the iron, he had to tap them with his fingers, which were burning because he wasn't used to it.

"You act like you ain't never do this before. You need me to get somebody to help you? I'll get somebody to help you, but I need the rest of that brick bagged up tonight. It's coming out there and I can't afford to stop the flow."

Chad couldn't relinquish his pride. He knew if anybody would have known that he was a bag up boy and in debt a hundred stacks that they would no longer think he was that dude, and more than anything he wanted people to think that he was that dude. Kenyan knew this and used it to his advantage.

****

"I'ma get with you later bro," Kenyan said dropping Terron off at his car. Terron had a Black Charger. He got in his car and headed to his grandmom house to stash some of the work, then he headed to the block.

"Y'all finish yet?"

"We were waiting on you," Z said.

"Where Juice and Reno?"

"Juice down the block on the porch."

"Go get him, I ain't trying to be standing here with this stuff on me."

Z went down the street and came back with both Reno and Juice. They gave Terron their money and he passed them both G packs. They still had a couple hours left to their shift, so they got to it.

"Let me taste something bro, I know you got something to smoke," Juice said.

"Of course, I do. You got something to roll it in," Terron asked?

"Yes sir, you know It," Juice said pulling a Dutch out of his pocket.

"You got a Dutch, you must got something to smoke."

"Nah, I was going to get something later but why wait later when you got something now," Juice said with a big smile on his face.

"You swear you be making sense, dumb ass! Give me that," Terron said snatching the Dutch out of his hand.

Terron twisted up while they posted on the block and smoked. The whole time Z, Juice, and Reno ran back and forth to their stash spots to bust traps.

Z and Juice was Terron's manz. Terron was fly with Reno, but he was more of Kenyan's and Kenny manz. He was in their age group. It was a lot of other dudes that trapped out there. Most of them were older than Terron, but they all respected him. That's why it was easy for him to run things for Kenyan.

"You seen Kenny," Terron asked Z?

"Yeah, he had some chicks in the car with him. He must was going somewhere, he gave Reno his gun to stash for him."

"He probably just went to a hotel," Terron said.

"Man, him and Chad be living that life," Juice said.

Terron was thinking only if Juice knew what he knew about Chad. He wasn't going to say anything though, he wasn't that type of dude.

"I'm trying to come through like them," Juice continued.

"We will, we just gotta play our part and stack this dough," Terron said passing Juice the Dutch.

A lot of traffic was coming through the block. Terron got up to look out for his dudes. Reno was in the street when he served these two black dudes in a Durango. He really didn't pay them any mind because as soon as he got done serving them, he had more fiends to serve. The rush was calming down, but Juice had his whole stash on him when the police came swarming from every angle. Everybody on the block ran, scrabbling, like ten dudes, even dudes who wasn't dirty ran. They caught Juice, checked his money and found the bills they sent their undercovers to purchase the drugs with.

****

Juice's sister opened the door after a few knocks.

"Hey Terron," she said smiling. Terron didn't pay her smiles any mind, he just asked where her mother was. "Mom, Terron is here for you," Joy yelled! She knew that he was there to get his mom so they could go bail her brother out of jail.

"Alright, tell him to give me a minute," she yelled back loud enough for Terron to hear.

"Tell her I'm going to be in ma car waiting," he said then went back to his car.

"Okay," Joy responded as she watched him walk away in admiration. She really liked Terron, but he didn't show any interest in her.

"She's coming," Terron told Kenyan when he got in the car.

Kenyan took out an air freshener to get the weed smell out of his car. He wanted to show Juice's mom some respect.

"This the kind of losses that I was talking about. Shit happens though. Even though you can't account for stuff like this, you still have to be prepared for it, feel me?"

Terron just nodded his head.

"What kind of person would I be if I just left him hanging? I'm saying he going to have to work that shit off though, I need all of mines," Kenyan said.

When Juice's mother came out Terron got out of the passenger seat and into the back. From there they went to go bail her son out.

****

The next day Juice came back to the block like it was nothing.

"Them county mats serious. Them things messed my back up I think," he said twisting his back.

"Man, you wasn't even in there for a day," Terron said.

"Shit, that's a lot when you never did a bid before.

Terron nor Juice had ever been locked up before. They both been in trouble with the law as juveniles, but nothing serious.

"You got something for me," Juice asked wanting some coke so he could start trapping. He knew that things didn't stop. The cost of a lawyer was an extra liability that he needed money for. Plus, he had to pay Kenyan back for bailing him out.

"Kenyan told me not to give you anything. He got something else for you to do. I think he going to have you bagging up, so you won't be out here making shit hot. You know them boys going to be on some bullshit if they see you back out here."

"I'm with that. I hope that's what he wants me to do. That way I ain't got to worry about getting cased up again. Ma mom was bugging out on me. You see she wasn't saying anything to me while we were in the car. When we got home, she was hitting me with all type of church stuff."

"I know that was blowing ya shit."

"Was it, that's ma mom so I ain't want to be ignorant. I had to tell her that I was going to get myself together. Get a job and start going to church. Now I gotta figure out how I'ma get out of that."

"Ain't no getting out of that unless you move out."

"For real, I might really have to do that."

"What you planned on living with ya mom forever?"

"No, just never really thought about it. Shit free there."

Terron knew what he meant, but he wasn't with that. He like to have his own. He was already in the process of getting his own apartment.

In the circle was half strip mall, but local stores mixed with residential housing. In the middle was a little park, but because of the drug activities, the kid's parents didn't allow them to play there.

****

Kenny stepped out of the barbershop looking like new money. He had a crispy cut. His waves were spinning like he just came home from prison. He never did a bid. He was just a pretty boy. He swagged down the block like it was his. While he might not have owned any property out there, half of the drugs that were being sold out there was his.

"What's good with the fellas," he asked as he walked up to Terron and Juice? After they greeted him back, he told Juice that he needed him to come with him.

Juice nodded his head. It was understood that he worked for Kenny and his brother. Him and Terron dapped each other and he got in the car with Kenny.

"Bro told me to come get you, he want you to bag up."

****

When they got in the house and went in Chad was sitting at the table bagging up. Something funny must have happened on tv because he was in the middle of cracking up when they walked in.

This dude bullshitting, Kenny thought to himself.

Chad tried to tighten up when Kenny came through the door. He was disappointed and ashamed when he saw Juice behind him.

"What is he doing here," he asked?

"Kenyan told me to bring him to the bag up spot. This the bag up spot, right," Kenny asked being sarcastic?

Chad was upset because he specifically told Kenyan that whoever he got to help him, not to bring them there with him. Then it occurred to him that he could have Juice do everything while he chilled.

"What's this right here," Kenny asked grabbing a bag of coke.

"That's 4 ½."

"I'ma take this, I got a sell for it. Show him what to do, I'm out."

Chad really wasn't feeling Juice being there or how Kenny was acting like bagging up was something he had to do. His pride was starting to get the best of him. When Kenny left Chad had Juice doing everything himself while he smoked, joked, ate snacks and watched tv. Juice didn't know that Chad was supposed to be bagging up with him. To him Chad was one of the big men on the block. He figured that he was just there making sure that he did things right.

After a few hours of being there not doing anything, Chad couldn't take it any longer. *They're not going to have me cooped up like a fucking animal,* Chad thought to himself before getting up off of the couch. "Yo, I'll be back in a little. I'm about to go handle something," he said leaving the house.

On his way home Chad had the music in his BMW X6 blasting. He rapped along with Meek Mills word for word while smoking his weed. He pulled up to his house and got out of his car. As he walked up the steps, he didn't notice the mask man creeping from behind the bushes that was next to the steps.

CRACK! Chad went out cold. When he woke up it was pitch black, he couldn't see anything. His head was throbbing with pain. He could feel that his mouth, wrist, and legs were taped up. He tried moving around, but was boxed in. He knew that he was in the trunk of a car from all the bumps and turns the car made as it rode. He could hear voices, but they weren't loud enough for him to understand what was being said.

He felt the car stop, then the doors shut like somebody got out of the car. Even though he was tied up and couldn't really do much he was thinking about what he was going to do to get out of that situation. He figured next time the truck opened he'll get to see who kidnapped him. That's not what happened though. He heard a door open and shut, then the car started moving. Suddenly it took a dive, then there was a splash. He was hoping and praying that what he knew was happening wasn't really happening. He knew it was though, and it was nothing he could do about it.

CHAPTER 4

Every day Terron woke up it felt surreal, like a never ending nightmare. Even if he did end up doing the rest of his life in prison, he could never get used to it. Even though the incident that happened in the mess hall didn't affect him, he still couldn't stop replaying it over and over in his mind. Even while he'll be trying to go to sleep it'll pop up. It was the topic among everybody, but the prison kept its regular movements. They were only lock down for that day.

"You alright youngen, you look a little down," Old head said to Terron.

"Nah, I'm good. I just got up."

"I hear you. Don't let what you saw get to you."

"I'm not, but that was some crazy stuff."

"Yeah, but I done seen it all. In prison you going to see all kinds of stuff. Just make sure you stay vigilant and be careful of who you deal with. You know how they say every brother ain't ya brother, well that's true."

"I could go with that. I'm about to use this phone right quick before they call us for rec," Terron said before stepping off. When he got to the phone Sham was on the phone right next to him spazzing on whoever he was talking to. He looked like he was stressed out. Terron could see it all in his eyes, but he had his own problems. He dialed his girl's number and the phone just kept ringing. He hung up the phone, then tried again only to get the same results. He became livid, because this was the second time he'd been trying to call and didn't get an answer. He knew at some point of the day she had to be there and wasn't doing anything. He couldn't help but to think that she wasn't picking up on purpose. He put the phone down disappointed. At the same time Sham was getting off of the phone, but when he was done, he slammed it on the hook causing the c.o. to look at him like he was crazy.

Sham was from Bergan County, one of the riches counties in the U.S... A lot of stars and rich people lived there instead of New York since it was so close. Home invasions was big out there. Terron didn't know if that was what Sham was locked up for, but he knew that he was serving fourteen years and had a murder charge pending that he was saying he didn't have anything to do with. Terron kind of believed him but it wasn't Terron who he had to convince. That murder case really had Sham stressed. Terron seen it and felt like he should say something.

"Yo bro, you know ya situation better than anybody, but if things ain't looking good for you go ahead and take something (Meaning a plea). Don't end up like me, some day light is better than none."

Sham heard him, but his mind was already set. He already had fourteen years. He wasn't trying to take anymore. Plus, he was adamant that he didn't have anything to do with it.

When rec was called out Terron went to the yard. It was always about a thousand people in the yard, spread out, doing some type of activity, rather illegal or recreational. The yard had everything in it from the football field that Sylvester Solon played on in that movie (Lock up), to basketball courts, volleyball courts with sand, a weight pile, handball court, Bocce Ball, to a track. Dudes did everything out there, including sell and use drugs.

When Terron got out there, his Muslim brothers were offering prayer. He went over there with them. They were deep but because they weren't in a religious setting they could only offer prayer six at a time. Anything else would have been group demonstration.

Terron salamed the brothers then went to sit with his manz.

"You playing ball today," Abdullah asked?

"Nah, I'm chilling. They can have that today. I'm going over there to watch though."

Terron and Abdullah got in the ranks and offered prayer. When they were done they started walking over to the basketball court, but decided to stop at the card table to talk to some of their peoples from Camden.

"Ya'll gambling," Abdullah asked?

"Nah," Ali responded.

"Let me get next then."

"You got that. Hold up, I know you not trying to cheat me," Ali said to the dude sitting across from him. It was four of them playing spades. Terron was just watching, he didn't plan on watching them for too long though.

"I ain't trying to cheat you," dude shot back.

"Alright, don't make me beat you how Kas beat that white boy."

"Fuck outta here. Yo, he went dumb, how you going to kill somebody over some cigarettes when you supposed to go home in eighteen months."

"For real, he done. They going to smoke his boots," another one of the dudes playing said.

"You know that he was taking meds, right? He better try to use that as his defense."

"Them mothafuckas not trying to hear that."

Terron stood there listening to the fakeness. Just not too long ago Kas was their manz. They were laughing and joking with him, now they were kicking his back in. Real dudes didn't do stuff like that. He knew that there was a reason why he didn't deal with this group of dudes like that. When the subject switched to what such and such on the streets got and was doing Terron spent off. The last thing he cared about was what another man was doing. One thing Kenyan taught him was watch out for the little fake stuff because it was a sign of something bigger to come.

Prison is full of guys like that, sitting around in groups gossiping like bitches. Terron felt like he was above that. He had too much on his mind to get caught up in prison politics.

Prison for Terron was something foreign. While other dudes were running around with smiles on their faces, Terron was nonchalant about everything. He spoke to people and kept it fly but he didn't do too much socializing. He mostly stayed to himself. He talked a lot to his Muslim brothers. Even though it was all love he still felt like a stranger amongst them.

Throughout his bid he seen some things that made him lose a lot of respect for dudes that call themselves grown men. His faith in God is what kept him going. It's many guys in prison that may not ever see the streets again, but they still find ways to keep their heads up. Rather it's through faith or hope. For Terron it was both because he was always in touch with his lawyer, even working on his case himself.

CHAPTER 5

"Come on now, I have to go," Terron said backing out of the house.

"You going to come back tonight," Suki asked while grabbing the front part of his belt?

"I told you I'm coming back."

"Alright, let me get a kiss," she demanded.

Terron leaned in giving her a kiss, then backed out of there just in time to escape her grasp.

Kenyan was impatiently waiting. He was looking through the passenger window at them. Beep Beep!

Terron broke away and headed down the steps to the car. Kenyan kept looking at Terron's girl like he knew her.

"What's good bro," Terron said as he got in the car?

"What's up. A yo, is that Suki?"

"Yeah, why, you know her?"

"Who don't, just have fun with her, don't make that ya girl."

"What you know about her?"

"I'm saying, she gets around. I know a few dudes that hit. She tries to deal with dudes who she think is doing something or who got potential. She ain't about nothing though. Do she be hitting you up for money?"

Terron really didn't want to answer that question. The look on his face gave Kenyan the answer.

Kenyan just smirked, "Ah she fucking and sucking you all crazy, got you coming out of ya pockets. Kenyan was laughing at him.

"You crazy as hell. I don't be giving her nothing."

"Stop lying, even I give ma chicks money. Now you going to sit here and tell me that you don't' be coming up off of anything?"

Kenyan knew Suki was a little older and was probably trying to take advantage of the situation. He wanted to know.

"I'm saying, I throw her a bone every now and then," Terron confessed.

"I knew it, I knew I was going to get it out of you. Don't let her vet you bro."

"I ain't."

"By the way I lied, I don't be giving ma broads nothing. Only ma girl. She the only one that might be there when I need her. All the other ones if they not enjoying it with me, they're assed out. I know they not going to be there for me when I need them. I seen it happen too many times."

While Kenyan was talking his phone began vibrating. "Yo," he said answering it.

"Bro, you need to get around here. Chad just got fished out of the river."

Kenyan couldn't believe what he was hearing. If it was true he knew who did it, but he really thought their word was good. All sorts of stuff was going through his mind. On his way to meet his brother he filled Terron in on what he had just heard.

****

"It's been on the news all day today. They pulled his car out of the river. He was duck tapped in the truck. They didn't say if he was shot or anything. They just said that he drowned," Kenny said looking at his brother.

Kenyan put his head down looking to the floor in thought.

"You think Raheem had something to do with it?"

"I don't know what to think right now. If he did I hope he don't expect me to pay that money. Hell no, he broke the deal."

"You right, we gotta get in touch with him to see what's up."

Chad was Kenyan's manz, but he wasn't feeling like somebody would be feeling after one of their close friends had just got murdered. Especially when they knew who did it. The way he seen it, Chad had brought that on himself. Kenyan was more worried about him not having to pay that money back.

****

Kenyan was in the bed sleep with his chick when he received a call.

"Yo," he said answering the phone.

"It's me bro, I need to talk to you about that. Meet me downtown in fifteen minutes."

Kenyan hung up the phone and called his brother to let him know that he was on his way to meet Raheem. He was kind of nervous. Even though Raheem was his brother in faith he still knew that in the hood you couldn't really trust anybody. As he got dressed, he tucked his gun on his hip for safe keeping. Every gangsta felt safer with their gun than without it. Every one of them feared the day that they might get caught without it. That's why the saying goes it's better to get caught with it than without it. The realest logic for someone who live that life is that they rather do five to ten than be carried by six.

Kenyan arrived at the spot that he was supposed to meet Raheem at, but there was no site of Raheem. That made him feel uneasy. There was a building across the street with a dark alley way next to it. He kept looking over there. Then a shadowy figure emerged out of the darkness. Kenyan took his gun off his hip and posted up near his car.

"It's me bro, come this way," Raheem said.

Relieved a little but not at all relaxed, especially not after what they did to his manz. He put his gun back on his hip and hesitantly began walking towards the alley way, still looking both ways he was hoping this wasn't a set up.

Raheem led him through that alley to another, then they ended up in a house.

"Look bro, I know you probably feeling some type of way about ya manz, but that wasn't done on purpose. Some on the younger brothers who didn't get the word in time had caught him slipping. They thought it was still money on his head."

Kenyan listened, it made since. He didn't think that Raheem would go back on his word. He was willing to forgive and forget, especially if they wasn't going to be expecting him to pay that debt.

"The Sheikh sends his regards. I know it ain't no bringing him back, but the Sheikh said you don't have to worry about that money. In fact, he said to give you something for your troubles. He likes you and want to keep doing business with you. That's on the Sheikh," Raheem said handing Kenyan a bag. "That's on the Sheikh. Come see me when you're ready to re-up."

Raheem walked him back to his car. Kenyan didn't look in the bag until he felt like he was safe. When he seen them bricks in there he was souped up. He had to pull over to see exactly how many was in there. He couldn't believe it. Instead of being in debt a hundred thousand he was up two bricks which was at least a hundred and twenty thousand once he sent it to the block. He wasn't even thinking about Chad's death anymore.

When Kenyan got to Kenny's house, he could tell that his brother was happy to see him. He gave him a strong man hug as soon as he opened the door.

"I'm glad to see that you good bro, for real. If anything would of happened to you, I was going to wild out. Look," Kenny said showing His brother the vest he had on and the AK 47 he had on standby. "I was going to go all in."

Kenny was the pretty boy of the two, but it wasn't anything that he wouldn't do for his brother. Kenyan felt the same way.

"That shit wasn't about nothing."

"What was he talking about?"

"He said the Sheikh wanted to apologize. Some youngens had got to Chad before the word could get to them that the hit was off."

"Dam, that's crazy. I wonder who got to him."

"I have no idea. All I was worried about was that money I agreed to pay."

"What he say about that?"

"He said everything good, not to worry about it. He even sent us something for our troubles," Kenyan said holding up the bag.

Kenny took the bag out of his hands and looked through it. "He gave you this on the muscle?"

"Yeah, he wanted to keep our business relationship alive."

"Who is this Sheikh dude he keep talking about, did you ever see him?"

"Nah, but he gotta be Muslim if he keep calling him Sheikh."

****

"You ready for what I told you? That debt squashed now that Chad dead, so I ain't going to bullshit you. See a lot of dudes be on some selfish shit, like they don't want their manz to come up. They want to be the leader. They want to be the only ones getting money. Them type of dudes are petty and insecure. That's one of the reasons dudes be getting crossed, killed or told on. You supposed to show ya real ones love. If I'm getting it, I want you to be eating as well, feel me?"

"Whatever you could move, I got you. You could put up to two trappers on the morning and night shift. You could still run the 4 to 11 or I could get someone else. That's up to you. I know you got other dudes from the city who want to buy something. You could front them, give them packs, whatever, just get money."

Kenyan was filling Terron's head with all kinds of ideas. All Terron could think about was how he was about to go in. He had a bunch of dudes he knew throughout the city who he could serve.

Terron bought a half of brick and was fronted the other half. He played with many bricks before but none of them was his. After he bought it, he admired it. It being his seemed like it had a different feeling to it. He had a sense of ownership, like a first time homeowner. Nas wasn't lying when he said a drug dealer's destiny was reaching a key, but Terron wasn't about to just settle for one.

Kenyan had the circle banging. Kenny became more of the guy who sold weight. He started off small, but he was social and dealt with a lot of people, so his flow grew fast. Kenyan was the opposite when it came to dealing with people.

Three bricks plus the coke Kenyan was already buying put them up. The circle was banging, and Kenny was selling a lot so Kenyan was copping more and more every time he went to re-up.

CHAPTER 6

Anwar's private jet finally landed after a twelve hour flight. Anwar got off the plane and was greeted by eight Muslim brothers dressed in all white with red and white turbans on. They shook hands, hugged and kissed cheeks as costumed in their country. Anwar smiled and spoke fluent Arabic with them as they walked towards the convoy of exotic cars that awaited them.

They rode through the desert for what seemed like an hour before they hit a city. No matter how many times Anwar been to Dubai he was always astonished by the beautiful architectural designs. It was like a different world, like the past brought into the future. The best part for him was that he was surrounded by peace loving Muslims.

The convoy arrived at the Burj Khalifa, the tallest building in the world. Every time he seen it the movie Mission Impossible came to mind. Anwar did most of his talking to the brothers on the ride to the hotel. They were to meet later for dinner. Until then he needed to get some shut eye. He walked through the seven star hotel looking at all the Muslims from every walk of life. He always wore his Muslims attire. For the most part he was dressed like every man there, just with his own twist to it. Instead of a turban he wore a kufi.

****

"Terron, can I have some money," Suki asked?

Terron was sitting on the edge of the bed counting stack after stack when he heard the question. He gave her a look that didn't need words, but she seen it before and knew that it didn't mean that she wasn't going to get what she wanted.

"Didn't I just give you $1,300 when we were in Nieman Marcus for that Christian Louboutin purse?"

"Yeah, but I wonna buy some shoes."

"All them shoes you got in that closet, you better wear a pair of them. You always wanting something, you better get a job."

She didn't even respond to his comment about her getting a job. She just stood there with her hand on her hip looking at him. She had a dress on so tight that one could see her heartbeat. Her hair was done, and she had heels on. She was looking like money, all on Terron's expense.

"Please Terron, I'm trying to get these red bottoms. You know how you like to fuck me with my heels on."

Suki was definitely right. She knew that he loved her in some heels. When she wore heels, she walked like a stallion on its hine legs, and her ass sat up crazy. Still Terron knew that she was getting out of control. She was trying to ball harder than him with his money. He gave in though.

"How much you need?"

"Eight hundred."

Terron tossed her a stack so she could get out of his face. She kissed and hugged him and immediately ran out of there like a little kid who finally had gotten their way. He shook his head in disgust as he watched her walk away in gold digger fashion.

It's like the more money she see I'm getting, the more money she want. I gotta stop bringing ma bread around her, Terron thought to himself. Then he remembered what Kenyan once told him. "Don't let that chick vet you." (Vet was short for Veteran. Someone who is experienced, that has been there and knows how to manipulate the situation to their benefit in whatever expect of life, rather male or female.) That's when he realized that he was being vetted. *Yeah, she gotta go,* he thought to himself.

Terron wasn't really into Suki for her to be peeling him for cash like that. She was just convenient. From day one she pushed up on him and that led to an almost year long relationship. At the end of the day, after he got finish running the streets, chasing money, messing with chicks or whatever she was always there looking good and willing to let him do whatever freaky thing to her that came to his mind. Plus, she knew how to treat him. He was so into his own world that he didn't care to know what she was doing when she went out.

Instead of renting an apartment like he was going to Terron had got his aunt to mortgage a house in her name for him and he moved Suki in with him.

CHAPTER 7

It was count time, Terron was locked in his cell probably the angriest person in that prison. Even though a lot of guys probably didn't get their visits that day none was more disappointed than Terron. Suki had told him that she was going to come visit him that Sunday. He had gotten a haircut the day before, took an early morning shower, was smelling fresh with Muslim oils, and had his crispy state clothes on. The ones he only pulled out when he knew he was going to get a visit. Him being stood up was like someone being stood up on a date, but these visits meant so much more. He never hit Suki before, but how he was feeling at that moment, he felt like doing her worse than Chris Brown did Rihanna.

He laid there with one leg on the bonk and the other still on the floor, one hand behind his head and the other rested on his stomach, just staring at the ceiling. He sighed deeply. The stuff he was thinking about could cause one to have a heart attack. Reality was setting in. He knew that people were acting funny because they thought that he was never coming home. The part that was killing him was that he couldn't do anything about it.

He haven't heard from Kenyan or any of his supposed to be dudes in months. That was another story, something else he was going through, but tried not to think of it because at the moment he had this chick on his mind. At the age of twenty six he felt like he didn't even know what stress was. He didn't even think he was stressing when he caught his charge or got convicted. Now he laid there thinking about the lack of love he was getting from the people who were supposed to be his love ones. Even his family wasn't keeping in touch with him the way they used too. That frustrated him because he did a lot for them. His aunt had his money, so she was his main outside contact. Everybody else the more time he had in the more they fell off.

After finishing with his stressful thoughts Terron finally sat up and turned his tv on. He heard the c.o. coming around with the mail. He turned around when the c.o. got to his gate. The c.o. put a book catalog on his gate. To Terron that wasn't mail. He wanted to hear from the streets. Not getting any mail only added to the frustration. *This ain't a good day, he thought to himself.*

"You got legal mail too. Get it on ya way to the mess hall," the c.o. said before stepping off.

"Alright," Terron responded.

"He was looking forward to a decision from his appeal. He knew that legal mail had to be it. He tried not to get his hopes up because he'd been through this on his first appeal, but this one him and his lawyer was almost certain that he would get him back in court. He had all the right grounds. Everything was showing clearly in black and white how they railroaded him.

When they called mess out, he went down to the mess hall.

"Who came to see you bro," Ali asked seeing him still with his crispy state clothes on?

"I ain't get no visit," he answered feeling some type of way. He got his tray, sat down and had to listen to other dudes talk about their visits. In the summertime during visits some guys were actually getting quickies in with their chicks, getting head and everything. Terron never got to experience an outside visit because when summer came around, he could never get in touch with Suki or any of his peoples. When she did eventually come up again it was winter.

It seemed like all the Camden dudes went out there except him. He couldn't help but to feel some kind of way. As far as hood status them dudes were nobodies compared to him. He was that dude. At least that's how he felt, but his peoples falling off on him was proving otherwise.

When mess was over hundreds of guys were trying to leave the mess hall at once. The cage only fitted a certain amount of people. Once it was full and dudes were packed in like sardines the c.o. would lock them in then open the other side of the cage to let them out.

One c.o. was tapping the cage with this metal thing to call dudes like they were cattle. This prick controlled the gate. He was always trying to slam it on whoever the last guy was. Terron was looking at him trying to catch dudes squeezing in. He was racist for sure. The hate in him showed by how hard he tried to muster the strength to violently slam the gate on people.

Bloom! One dude got hit and bounced back. He tried again as the c.o. hit him again before dude got in. The c.o. put on a little devilish grin and looked at the black LT., but the LT. looked like he didn't approve of his actions. He just didn't say anything.

"Look, that made his day," Terron told Ali as he shook his head. He never tried to squeeze in the gate because he knew if he was to get hit with that gate like that he was going to trip out.

"Yo, I gotta go get this legal mail. I'ma get up." Terron went to the property room, got his mail, then went back to his tier. He didn't want anyone seeing his facial expressions if things didn't go his way. In his cell he opened it, simultaneously praying. Without reading his eyes scanned the letter while hoping for the best, but there it was in big bold red letters. DENIED! After seeing that the rest of the letter was irrelevant. Still, he stared at the paper as if his eyes were playing tricks on him, nothing changed though. He read the rest of the letter to see what the reason was.

He knew he did what he did, but he also felt like they messed up so he should be able to give some time back. The law was the law, and they were supposed to follow it too. He had case law for every issue he was bringing up. The facts were clear cut, but they still denied him. He realized how true that saying was. (It was easy to come to prison, but hard to get out). The denial of his appeal was another blow that made him feel like this could possibly be where he would spend the rest of his life. He told himself he wouldn't give up though.

Every Friday he went to Jummu'ah (Islamic Service) to hear the sermon. It was always motivational, and it helped him get through the rest of his week on his Deen. Today for some reason he had to force himself to get up, he felt drained of energy. He didn't feel like doing anything, including going to Jummu'ah. A part of him felt hopeless and wanted to deal away with everything and everyone. The other part of him wanted to leave his cell and knock out the first person he saw. He had to check himself. He knew that them kind of thoughts were a sign of weakness. He was stronger than that.

Only weak people lose control. The strong stay in control, dominate their mind and emotions and make the best out of whatever situation. Terron collected his energy, got himself together, and trooped it out. With all the time guys had in that prison, he definitely wasn't the only one feeling how he was feeling.

The Iman gave a good hour long khutbah (sermon). It ended around 2:30 in the afternoon. Afterwards dudes went back to their prison affairs, talking about this and that.

"What's good Akhi," Quick said as he walked over to where Terron was at?

"What's good," Terron responded? Him and Quick was fly. Even though Quick was Muslim he was blood too. That's why he never really gave dudes the salaams unless they gave it to him first. He didn't know how dudes seen him because some brothers didn't like or allow people to be in the ranks if they weren't just Muslim. In that prison half of the population was Muslim and most of them had allegiance to other things outside the folds of Islam. Latin Kings, Crips, Blood, Niyetas, or dudes just being loyal to the block they were from. Throughout every other thing that It was, Muslims were the majority. It's what kept the peace between everybody else.

"I want to talk to you when we go outside later," Quick said with a grin on his face. He was always up to something, which was why he was always locked up. He was one of them dudes who been jailing since he was a juvenile. He was currently serving time for a body. Because he served time most of his life, everyone knew him from prison. That's where his reputation was built and that's what he was known for. He spent his bid reading books like, The 48 Laws of Power and The Art of War, but was never able to implement them outside of prison. He knew that Terron was thorough from how he moved and everything he heard about him. Still, in his mind he seen a soldier, and to him every soldier needed a general. That's what he seen himself as. The Master mind, the manipulator, a strategist, but one thing about people who always think they're smarter than other people is that they underestimate other people. Terron was a young vet.

"Alright," Terron replied. He already knew what he wanted to talk to him about.

****

Later that day Terron was chilling outside with a few Camden dudes laughing and joking. When Quick came over there with them the whole vibe changed and Terron could feel it. At the time not too many dudes from Camden were gang banging so they wasn't feeling it. Therefore, they weren't really feeling Quick. One by one dudes started dispersing. Quick knew dudes wasn't feeling him, but he acted like it was nothing to him. It's not that he wasn't a thorough dude because he was. It was just his aura. The sly, manipulative, insincerity was all over him and he wasn't even manipulating anyone, but it was the fact that people could tell that he was always trying. He was basically see through.

Terron knew how to jail off of dudes like him. People who always thought they were master minding something. It was plenty of dudes like him in prison, and in life in general. After all the other dudes peeled off, Terron and Quick started walking the track talking.

"You alright," Terron asked Quick seeing how he kept looking around, not nervously but like he wanted to make sure he was on point?

"Yeah, I'm good. I just dropped ma flag and told ma manz that I'm not dealing with them no more. It was too many muts and snitches under that set. I'm good, but I don't trust these dudes. They might try to sleepwalk me."

While he was talking Terron was hoping that nothing went down while they were together. He wouldn't know if he should help or not. He didn't want to get involved in something he didn't have anything to do with. That didn't make him a punk, it made him smart. Now if Quick wasn't with that and they were walking the track and dudes tried to ride out on him, then Terron a ride out with him until the sun burnt out.

"Right now I'm in the middle of switching my set. I'm in touch with a couple dudes from Cali, so I got a few options. I'm just waiting for everything to play out then I'm going to decide. That's why I wanted to get with you because I'm starting from the bottom up. In this shit I don't want any muts, or rats. Only thorough dudes that's about something. I did my homework on you and only got good responses. I know you solid from the way you move. That's why I want you to be a part of what I'm putting together."

"You talking about becoming blood?"

"Yeah."

"Nah bro, I'm good. You ma peoples but I can't deal with them other dudes."

"You ain't got to deal with them other dudes. Why you think I fell back from them. I'm talking about building something on some Mafioso shit."

"We can do that without dealing with that."

"But this is already established. Plus, I got dudes all over that's with this that I'm connected to."

He was talking about dudes who he was writing in other prisons all over the country. None of whom he actually met, basically pen pals. Terron seen through all of this, but he listened as Quick tried to convince him. Quick was trying to make it seem like some mob stuff. That was far from the reality Terron seen from his prison experiences. To him it looked like grown men playing little kid games with their lives. He seen very few, if any that were moving right. When there was some, they were the dudes all the rest were looking up to.

Quick started naming certain dudes from Camden that Terron knew that started dealing with that. He was right, eventually the gang stuff did hit Camden, but the dudes who he was naming was guys who had been locked up their whole lives. They never really had a life on the streets. Prison was their influence, that's how they fell victim to it. He couldn't really name anybody who was about something, who got money, or who really counted on the streets except one person. Even that person really didn't count, he just had money, but he talked about him like that was his trump card.

Quick was talking about some dude name Nutty from A.V.. He had the front of A.V. on smash and got brought home when he was locked up. When he went home all his dudes became what he was since he was their leader anyway. He eventually caught an indictment and snitched, then all the dudes who was under him became food.

For the remainder of rec Terron listened as Quick ran down the history and politics of what he dealt with.

CHAPTER 8

When Anwar got back to the states, he made one phone call to Raheem, letting him know that he was back. To Raheem that meant more than what he just said. He went and got his squad. A couple of them jumped in the rented Penske truck while a couple rode with Raheem. They rode for hours to a rural area with cows stinking up the air. They pulled on to a private landing strip where a jet awaited them. The jet door opened. A guy said something to Raheem and they got to unloading the plane.

Anwar was to a point that he didn't see the coke anymore. He seen the money, that's all. Raheem was his go to guy. Through him he served some of the biggest drug dealers on the east coast. Practically half of the coke flowing through Camden came from him one way or another, most didn't know it. He only talked business with Raheem and another brother that he'd been serving for a while name J-Mills. Through them he moved everything. Even though he had guys around him that played certain roles, like his bodyguard, hit men, dudes he sent to do this and that, them dudes were the only two he talked coke with. He trusted that if things were to ever get ugly that they would hold up. Dude J-Mills had already proven himself before when he had caught an indictment and didn't turn state. He ended up beating the charges.

As soon as Raheem got the product back to Camden, he started making moves, shipping them out. From the most to the fewest. Raheem had a tight squad. They moved out like a well oiled machine. Most dudes buying from him didn't know about Anwar at all, but Raheem would sometimes make reference of the Sheikh, creating this larger than life figure that dudes came to fear and hold reverence for. They respected Raheem, his movement, and their squad so for him to hold him up and have things the way they were he had to be that dude.

****

Kenyan and his dudes were getting money. The more they got the more they balled out, the more haters envied them. Kenny had dudes wanting to get at him because he was always smashing their chicks. This night a few of them decided to go hang out at a local bar. White Boy Fairview wasn't necessarily known for breading thorough dudes so when they came through the downtown dudes who was in there deep seen potential victims. Every hood had hyenas, dudes that couldn't get their own, so they wanted the next man's.

That's how these particular downtown dudes were. They was in the bar deep, and none of them had intention on scooping a chick and leaving with them for the night.

Kenny was chilling on the wall talking to some chick. She was blushing, he definitely had her. Every move he made caused the light to reflect off of his diamonds. Rather it was his earrings, chain, watch, whatever, he was looking like money. He was so much into entertaining his new lady friend that he didn't see the dude creep up on him. Dude tried to snatch Kenny's chain, but it didn't pop. Kenny turned around punching on dude. Terron started helping, but downtown dudes swarmed them, smashing them out. They ran their pockets and took everything that was shinny on them. They went in the bar looking like money, but left looking like beat up bums. The good thing was that none of them was seriously hurt.

****

"Yo you good bro," Kenyan asked Terron?

"Hell no," I'ma body one of them."

"Chill bro, don't talk like that on the phone. I'm on my way over there."

When Terron opened the door for Kenyan he had two black eyes and a busted lip.

"Dam, they fucked you up," Kenyan said smirking. He wanted to laugh but held it in.

Terron tried to laugh too, but almost bust the stiches in his lip.

It's been three days since that club ass whopping. Terron took them days to heal up. He had too much pride to show up in the hood looking how he was looking. Out of everybody he had got it the worst.

"What's up with ya brother? I was talking to him about getting back at dudes and he was telling me to chill, just leave it alone. How am I supposed to leave this alone," Terron asked pointing to his face? "I got trashed trying to shoot him some bail and he talking about chill. What's up with him?"

"That's him, he don't want no drama. He just want to get money and mess with the broads. You gotta understand that everybody not built for the same stuff. It's like a sports team. Certain dudes play certain positions. You have to let dudes play the position their good at. If somebody playing the wrong position their going to be ass, and the team going to end up losing. That's why I got him selling weight. He good with people and he deal with a lot of dudes. On the other hand, if anything goes wrong, like somebody rob him or don't wonna pay up, that's when I go in. See what I'm saying?"

"Yeah, I hear you," Terron responded.

"I need you to do more than hear me. I want you to comprehend and implement this shit into ya life. This game I'm feeding you. Dudes be out here their whole life winging it and be wondering why they never progress. It's because they either was taught wrong, or they weren't taught at all. Best believe I ain't going to leave you hanging though baby boy, I got you. Until death do us a part, you little bro," Kenyan said rubbing Terron's head, messing up his waves.

"Come on man," Terron said trying to smack Kenyan's hand, but he had already moved it. Terron hated when Kenyan did that.

"I feel you though. They ain't getting away with that. One thing you never take is an L, reputation is everything. If we let something like that go other dudes are going to start coming at us thinking we're sweet. That's why I did my homework and found out where dude Maze live. He supposed to be one of their big men, they listen to him. He lives in the hood, but they be right down the street. So, what do you want to do?"

"It's whatever, I just need a couple more days to heal up. Feel like they tried to break ma back."

"Alright, say no more."

****

Doom! The door kicked in, the two masked men came through it holding what at the moment seemed like the biggest guns in the world. The dude who was on the couch sat there looking up in awe. The Draco flipped him over the couch. The other dude tried running but got tore up before he could even start. Maze came down the steps with a gun in his hand like he was about to do something, but never got a chance to use it. The shots hit his body causing him to tumble down the steps. After murdering them three they headed towards the back of the house where they seen a chick underneath the table balled up. They couldn't see her face. She knew they were there. She was praying that they didn't kill her. Since she never showed her face her life was spared. They held their guns on her as they backed out of the kitchen. If at any point she would of lifted her head up she would have loss her life. After riding out a couple of blocks they both took their mask off.

"That was good stuff, you sure that was ya first time? You moved out like a vet."

Terron tried to laugh but the nervousness and adrenaline had him paralyzed. He leaned back in his seat and started taking deep breaths. It was really his first time, he couldn't believe it went down how it did. It was too easy and it felt empowering. He took off his gloves and looked at his trembling hands. He smiled, leaned back against the chair and folded his hands on his stomach.

"You can never tell anybody about this bro. No matter what. Ain't no statute of limitations on murder, and in this shit you can't trust anyone. Sometimes ya best friends become ya worst enemy. When that happen, they'll use everything they know about you against you. We take this shit to the grave with us. Our peoples don't even need to know. All they need to know is to be on point."

Kenyan pulled up along Terron's car. "Get rid of that burner. I'll get up with you tomorrow."

"Alright bro."

Terron got rid of his burner and went home. He still had the jitters a little but was feeling like a different person. Even though he got away, he was still nervous. It was always a thought if anybody would know what they just did.

Suki was in the bed sleep when he got in the room. He cuddled up to her spooning. His movement woke her up. She felt him on her butt and got wet. She turned around and began kissing him. She slid her panties down and they began having sex.

"Yes baby, it's all your daddy," Suki whispered as she humped back. "I love this dick, you know how to treat this pussy. Oh my god."

Every few strokes she was whispering something sweet in his ear, which encouraged him to go harder and longer. When he was about to come he put her legs on his shoulders and started jack hammering the pussy. She couldn't say anything then, she just held him as tight as she could as he raced to get it all out.

CHAPTER 9

Let me see that 2:C book Terron said to the paralegal dude behind the counter. Dude grabbed the book and sat it on the table.

"What's up Crunch," Terron said to the other paralegal who was back there. Crunch was always in the Law Library working on his case. He was locked up for burglarizing Patrick Ewing's house in Bergan County New Jersey. He had came off with a lot of money and goods, but when he got caught they gave him 50 with a 25 year sentence. Him and Terron was on the same tier, so they talked often.

"Where Sham at," Terron asked Crunch?

"He went to court the other day."

"That's why I haven't been seeing him."

"He been gone for a couple of days now. I think he starting trial."

They kept their conversation short because the paralegal Terron used came out and they began talking. The paralegal he used always made Terron do everything himself, that way he'll learn. When Terron first asked him for help he told him that he'll help him for free, but he wasn't going to do the work for him. Terron's generation wasn't like his, it was hell of guys with life, or twenty years and better, but only a few in the Law Library trying to get home. Instead, they rather be in the big yard politicking with their manz who was eventually going to go home and forget about them.

Terron had already put another appeal in. He was waiting to hear something. With the court system everything was a waiting process. In there guys didn't have any choice but to develop some patience. Nothing was on their terms, that's one of the things that always ate Terron up.

Later that night he hit the yard where he ran into Quick.

"I got something to show you," Quick said.

They walked over to the handball court and sat on the ledge. Quick pulled out some pictures and handed them to Terron.

"These all dudes, where the broads at?"

"Nah, this ma manz and them from Cali. That's who I be dealing with. That's who going to give me my own hood."

Terron was looking at the pics, but he wasn't impressed. It was just a bunch of dudes in prison like them.

"That's ma manz and the rest of them are under him."

Quick was bigging dude up like he was really somebody. Terron couldn't understand how somebody as thorough as quick could let someone all the way on the other side of the country son him out and be telling him what to do.

"Yo, let me ask you a question bro. Why you waiting for somebody in California to give you something. Whatever they're doing you could do without them. What do you need this dude for," Terron asked giving him his pictures back?

"This shit official bro. You don't understand, with this I'm really connected. I know dudes out there, I could go out there right now and they'll embrace me like I'm family. I got a few states I can go to and get that kind of love. It's all about being connected. Dudes is doing big things and I want in. When certain dudes I know come home, if dudes ain't moving on this we moving them out. That's how it's going to be, I'm telling you. Me and ma dudes already politicked on it. We all dudes who been down for fifteen or better and we trying to eat."

Quick was adamant about how he was on it, but Terron knew that he would be in for a rude awaking if he thought that things were going to be that easy. Him and his dudes had been down for a long time. Dudes on the streets was established and wasn't going to be trying to hear somebody trying to push up on them.

CHAPTER 10

"Until death do us apart bro," Kenyan yelled over the loud music. He held his glass up giving Terron a toast then drunk the shot real fast. "Let me get another shot of that Remy," he told the bar tender slamming the shot glass on the counter and pushing it towards her. "Until death do us a part," Kenyan reiterated to Terron. Terron shook his head, he knew his manz was pissy drunk, he knew how he was when he was drunk.

Nobody knew that Kenyan and Terron committed them murders. Them downtown dudes had enemies all over. Of all of their beefs the least likely they would have expected was dudes from White Boy Fairview. They must didn't know the principle to never underestimate your enemy.

"Come on, let's get out of here," Terron suggested.

"Hold up, let me snatch one of these chicks up. That Remy got me wanting to punish something." Kenyan eyes scoured the bar. It was way too many options. He just grabbed the closest chick.

"What's up shorty, you trying to come with me?"

When Terron seen who he went up to, he just shook his head. The chick was short, fat and busted. Terron knew that she wasn't his manz type and if he wasn't drunk, he wouldn't have been pushing up on her. He went over there to stop him.

"Never mind him, he's drunk," Terron said to the chick who was sitting there blushing.

"Nah bro, I got this. She coming with me," Kenyan insisted.

"You sure," Terron asked?

"Yeah."

"Let me get ya keys. I can't let you drive home like that." Terron knew that if he was going to leave with her out of all the chicks that were there then he was definitely vision impaired and that it was a strong possibility he could get into an accident. He couldn't let him go out like that.

"Go to ma House," Kenyan said as the three of them got in the car.

Terron kept his mouth shut, but he was thinking dam, he about to take this scud bucket to his house.

"Loyalty is everything in this shit bro. I'm telling you, you ma bro. I'll do anything for you. I'ma always have ya back bro. I expect the same from you because that's how the real do. Don't no chicks supposed to come between us, or before ya manz. Straight up, no excuses when it comes to ya manz. We're bothers, I love you. No homo."

Terron knew that he was dead serious, but he couldn't help but to start laughing because of how Kenyan was saying it. The drunk expression on his face was looking crazy.

"Why you laughing bro, for real? You don't understand like, this shit real. You wouldn't be ma dude if I didn't trust you."

"I know man," Terron said.

The girl in the back seat giggled a little.

"See man, you think I'm playing," Kenyan said before dozing off.

"Wake up," Terron said nudging Kenyan's shoulder.

"I'm up I'm up, "Kenyan said looking around.

"Come on, you home."

Terron and the chick had got out of the car. Kenyan had dozed back off. Terron got him out of the car. Him and the girl carried Kenyan in the house and put him in the bed. Kenyan was knocked out. If Terron wasn't there o girl could have taken advantage of him.

"You want something to drink?"

"Yes, thank you," the girl said.

She was out of her league being with them. Terron didn't want to be ignorant to her. She kept looking at him. He felt her staring. He was thinking, *Should I hit that.* She wasn't his type, but then again, he didn't have a type for the type of chick he'll hit. To him pussy was pussy. Men always had a saying, pussy ain't got no face. It all depended on what time of day or night it was and how he was feeling that determined how his night ended.

He bought the chick over a Mountain Dew Soda, he also had one for himself. She quenched her thirst by taking a sip. He stood in front of her and unzipped his pants. She waited in anticipation for his manz to come out. She didn't ask any questions. She knew what to do with it. She sucked him off for a good five minutes. He stopped her and told her to take her clothes off.

She wasn't sexy at all, but he was rocked up and ready to punish something. Terron bent her over and started hitting it from the back. It never occurred to him that he was playing Russian roulette by hitting it raw. Terron trashed o girl for about twenty minutes. He got his and wasn't worried about if she got hers.

The next morning Kenyan woke up and came downstairs and seen Terron and the chick sleep on the couch together. He frowned up his face. "Where the hell did he get her from," he said to himself smiling as he went to the kitchen. A few minutes later Terron walked in there.

"You alright bro, you was bugging last night."

"I was bugging, look who you in there laid up with. You be hitting anything," Kenyan said.

"What! You the reason why she's here. You bagged her, came here and fell asleep so I ended up hitting it."

"Geeet the hell out of here! I know I ain't push up on that. I could have shampoo in ma eyes and still find a better chick to put ma dick in than that."

They both started laughing. O girl was in the other room playing like she was sleep, but she heard them in there clowning her. They had her feeling like shit on the inside.

"Don't let her looks fool you, she got some good pussy and good head," Terron said as they walked back in the living room.

"She probably do, but I don't want none of it. Come on, let's get out of here. I got shit to do."

CHAPTER 11

Terron sat back laughing as he thought about how him and his dudes use to do things. Good thing no one saw him because they probably would of thought he was crazy. He stayed reminiscing about the past. Him and his dudes had a lot of good times. After the laugh faded, he started having more serious thoughts, like the principles that Kenyan used to be teaching him. For the first time he realized that Kenyan didn't live up to any of that stuff he was talking about. It's been almost two and a half years since Terron heard from him. Every time he thought about it, he got pissed off. It was one of the reasons he couldn't deal with that stuff Quick was trying to put him on. He felt as though if his day one manz abandoned him, then imagine what these other dudes a do. He was loyal to his dudes and would have done anything for them, that's why he was locked up.

Since he wasn't getting the love he deserved he felt like he was loyal to a fault. He sat back thinking about what the old head said about loyalty being overrated. At first, he didn't agree, but now he was seeing what old head meant.

The thoughts that he might never go home again was hitting him hard. On top of that everybody had shitted on him. He tried not to let it eat him up but the thoughts that he might not ever see the other side again was stronger than anything.

The c.o. opened the gates and Terron walked to old head's cell.

"What's good youngen," old head asked?

"You know the usual, trying to get the white man foot off of ma neck."

"I hear that," old head responded.

"You know I finally got some time to dwell on that loyalty is overrated stuff that you was talking about."

"It's real, ain't it?"

"Yeah man."

"When you realize that loyalty is overrated you realize that them people you had love for and that was supposed to have love for you ain't shit. See youngen, I try to be about peace. I'm about black empowerment, but the truth is I know that dudes only respect violence, strength, and pressure and the white man knows that too, that's why he keep his foot on people neck. When you get the chance, you have to do the same thing because that's the only thing that's going to work. Why you think they get involved with all this nonsense. They want somebody to tell them what to do. You have to look at it like that to stay on top. Ain't nothing wrong with it. Just remember at the end of the day that don't none of them really give a fuck about you. Pardon my language."

Their conversation was broken up by the c.o. opening the main gate to let the tier out for mess. Terron felt like he could hear him talk that shit all day. How he was feeling, what old head was talking about, it was like he was talking to his soul.

As their tier was coming out so was another tier. Terron seen Sham and went over to speak to him. Sham turned around with blood shot red eyes. Terron knew something was wrong. When Terron spoke he didn't say anything back. He just had this blank stare. Terron didn't get offended, he kind of felt sorry for him. He went over to his peoples, and they walked to the mess hall.

"I heard he got life for that body," dude that was with Terron said.

"Yeah, that's why he looking like that, huh?"

Somebody getting life didn't shock Terron. He had life, so did a lot of other dudes in that prison.

"When he came back, they took him to the hospital. I don't know for what, but I think they got him taking medication now."

"Aye man, it don't matter how he do it, they still going to make him do it."

What Terron said was true for everybody in prison. A lot of guys tried to escape reality by using drugs, medications, or other avenues, but the truth was, there is no escape.

A few days later Terron was in the big yard talking to his manz Ace. They were walking the track when a code went off. All the c.o.'s started running to the visiting hall. A lot of dudes had posted up near the gate to find out what was going on. Terron and Ace didn't pay it any mind, but bout time they walked around the track and came back the c.o.'s were bringing some dude out all bloody. They were carrying him by his arms and legs off the ground. Everybody could tell that they had beat him bad. Dude manz was on the gate. Terron heard somebody say who it was, but he didn't catch the name.

While the c.o.'s were carrying him they counted to three then they all dropped him at the same time on his face. His manz who was in the big yard was heated, they began shaking the gate, yelling at the c.o.'s... The c.o.'s took about five more steps then dropped him again. That caused the dudes in the yard to really go berserk. Everybody in the yard was feeling for dude because they knew that it could have easily been one of them.

For the rest of the rec period Terron could see dudes were scheming, talking in secret about what they were going to do about the situation. Terron definitely wanted to see if dudes was built like that because dudes walked around all day tough towards one another, but when them pigs did something to them all that gangsta stuff went out the window. Plus, he knew that if it was another prisoner who would of did that to dude, it would have really went down.

When rec was up the c.o.'s let everybody in gate by gate. It wasn't hard to tell that something was about to go down. Terron and Ace made it in the gate right before the last gate. As soon as they got in their cells the sirens went off. They could tell that it was really going down because the sirens stayed on the whole time. When dude manz came from rec they walked through the tie two like everything was normal. Usually everybody would go either left or right to their tiers, but all dudes manz had slid over to three wing.

When the dudes had got to three wing there were three c.o.'s at and around the desk, Two white dudes and a black lady. They started beating the breaks off of the dudes. They lady had gotten hurt, but she didn't get it as half as bad as the dudes. She was the one who had pushed the code. Once the sirens went off, the dudes ran to the back to put their backs to the wall and rocked out. It was only eight of them. They rocked out for a little but at the end they lost.

The prison had got locked down. Being locked down really didn't bother Terron. He had everything he needed to jail with in his cell. The sergeant had called a dude to his office who he knew was affiliated with the others. Dude ended up beating the sergeant up.

For like a week straight codes were going off back to back. It seemed like every time they would let one of them dudes out it was going down. Then the SAG team got brought in. They're a special team of big cocky c.o.'s from every prison that get brought in to instill the order of things. They always ended up beating a few dudes up. Terron didn't know what they were doing because he was on four wing and it all was happening on three wing.

After about a month of being locked down the movement finally got back to normal. Dudes wasn't even talking about it anymore because it seemed so long ago. Plus, most were just happy to be outside of their cells again.

****

"What you know about this," Crunch asked Terron showing him a magazine.

"Dam, let me see."

Crunch gave Terron the Magazine. It was all chicks with fat asses in there. Terron flipped to the cover. Straight Stunten, it read.

"Where you buy this from? Let me get the info."

"This Sham shit, go ask him."

After flipping through the magazine, he knew he had to get a subscription. He gave it back to Crunch then went to Sham's cell.

"What's up Sham?"

"What's going on."

Sham was looking a little better than when he first came back from court, but everybody jailed with their problems differently.

"Let me get the information to that magazine you let Crunch see so I can order it."

"I have to find it for you. It's in here somewhere. I'ma send it to you."

"Alright, thanks, be easy" Terron said before leaving.

Later that night a runner came through and put the info on Terron's gate and told him that it was from Sham.

The next morning Terron woke up to keys jiggling. What he was hearing was the c.o. walking around doing his last count before shift change. Usually, Terron didn't wake up when the c.o. did his morning count, but this c.o. had his keys jiggling like a female and he was walking extra hard. As Terron laid there, he could hear him on all the way on the other side. All of a sudden, he heard the c.o. start running, then the code went off.

"That's Sham," Crunch said through the bars.

Nobody said anything. At first Terron didn't think much of it until Crunch said that, then he realized that the only code that could be going off that early was if someone tried to kill themselves, because four wing was single cells.

Come to find out Sham was in his cell hanging from the light fixture. The prison got locked down for a couple of hours. They got served breakfast in their cells, but when it was time for rec movement, things was back to normal and Sham was still in the cell hanging. They couldn't touch him for investigation reasons, so they just put a sheet up to cover the gate so no one could see him as they walked by.

"That's crazy how he hung himself," Mar said.

"It was that time. He couldn't handle them letters. I seen it in his eyes. He wasn't right after he came back from trial. That's messed up, I believe he really didn't do it."

"Dude in the cell next to him said he heard something sound like it fell over there last night."

"Dam, he was up there for a while," Terron said.

"It takes some balls to hang yaself," Man said.

"He had just sent me the info to that Straight Stunten magazine."

"That's probably why he hung himself. Them chicks in there are serious. It's hard to see stuff like that and think about how you never going to get pussy again."

CHAPTER 12

"You need these," Kenny asked Kenyan?

"Nah why," Kenyan asked?

"I got a sell for them. Fat Chop want to buy something. He practically begged me to sell him something. He see us eating now he want in. Before he used to just blow by us."

"You know how it is," Kenyan said too Kenny as he left out the door.

Kenny pulled up to Ferry Station where Fat Chop wanted to meet him. He pulled behind Fat Chop's car but didn't see him in it. Then out of nowhere Fat Chop appeared. Fat Chop got in the car with Kenny, and they made the transaction. Everything was everything until Kenny got to the corner and the feds swarmed him from every angle. Kenny was stuck looking at the unmarked cars swarm him, agents jumping out of their cars pointing guns at him. As soon as he seen the DEA jackets, he knew that he was set up.

"Hello," Kenyan said answering his phone.

Kenyan accepted the call immediately when he heard it was his brother.

"Hello."

"Yo bro, some bullshit happened."

"What you doing locked up?"

"Man, Fat Chop set me up."

"You sure it was him?"

"A hundred percent certain, as soon as I pulled off, they ran down on me. I got caught with everything. I see the judge tomorrow. I'll let you know what my bail is."

They stayed on the phone talking but wasn't saying anything particular. They knew them boys was more than likely listening. Kenyan was furious that his brother had gotten locked up. He was the one he depended on and trusted the most. Not to mention he knew that Kenny was going to end up doing some serious time.

The next day everybody from around the way was talking about Kenny's arrest. Terron was getting all of the twisted info that dudes who didn't know what really happened was saying. He called Kenyan trying to get the real scoop.

"I'll talk to you when I get there," Kenyan told him.

Later on Kenyan picked Terron up from some chick house out Fairview.

"What's up bro, everybody talking about what happened with Kenny."

"Yeah, they just gossiping, using somebody's else down fall as entertainment. You know how it go. Never mind that though. I got some work for you to put in. You think you can handle it?"

"I can handle whatever, just let me know what it is."

"It's dude Fat Chop. He the one who set Kenny up."

"That's the dude who be riding around here in that Black Audi, right?"

"That's him."

"Dam, he working with them boys, huh? I just heard somebody the other day bigging him up, talking about how much money he be getting. He puts together events and shows too, right? They said he got a comedy show coming up this weekend."

"He does stuff like that. You know that might be a good spot to get him, because he don't be around the hood like that so it's going to be hard to catch him slipping. Do you think you can get some tickets for that?"

"You already know. You can get anything for the right amount of money," Terron said.

"I'm bugging, you're definitely right. That's where we're going to get him at. I can't go, he see me, he going to know I'm on some bs."

****

Fat Chop had his event on a Sunday night. He rented a big Venue in Pennsauken. It didn't take long for the place to fill up. Fat Chop politicked with a lot of dudes who was getting money. He made sure they all showed up, which they did, to almost every event he put together. This gave the feds a chance to see who was who. Even though they weren't seen or heard, they were definitely there.

All the dudes that Fat Chop invited were pulling up in hot whips. Bentley's, Lambos, Ferraris, you name it. Some of them came with bad chicks attached to their hips, some knew they were going to leave with something bad. It was like date night, but it seemed like more ballers was out than any other time. Fat Chop was a known promoter. People from all over came to his events. For the past two months it also was being advertised on the radio.

Terron got out of his wheels Taylor made. He wasn't trying to stand out, he didn't need that kind of attention. Suki got out of the car complimenting his colors. Her heels had her as tall as him. Suki looked good, but it was so many bad chicks at that event that her ranking shot down a couple notches.

Kenyan was across the street in his car laid back in the seat when he seen Suki get out of the car. He shook his head laughing on the inside at his boy. No matter how good Suki looked he knew her history.

Terron had paid good money for his table. It was far right but close to the stage. He wanted to play the cut but also keep an eye on Fat Chop. They ordered some food and wine. Suki insisted on the wine. Terron was a Patron guy, he didn't really mind because he had a mission to complete. Drinking too much would only ruin things.

They sat there eating, drinking, laughing and enjoying the show. Fat Chop came out introducing every comedian himself, in between he threw his little corny jokes out there. He would end up laughing louder and harder than anybody in the crowd did. He was corny and either he didn't know it, or he didn't care. From where Terron was sitting he could see a little in the back.

"I'll be right back," he told Suki before getting up. Everyone was paying attention to the comedian on stage. The whole place was dim except the stage. He slid in the back unnoticed. There was a hallway with a couple of rooms. He figured them rooms must be where the comics get prepared at. He put his ear to one of them, he didn't hear anything. He looked at the door, it had the little man on it letting him know that it was the men's bathroom. Across the hall was the lady's bathroom. He heard someone come out of one of the other rooms, so he dipped into the bathroom. He peeked out and seen the person turn the corner. He went to the room the dude came out of. He peeked in and seen two of the comedians who had already performed. He kept going near the stage area where he seen Fat Chop near the curtains.

Another comic was just coming off stage. Fat Chop shook his hand and told him good job. He then went on stage, said a few stupid jokes and introduced the next comedian. When he was done, he came backstage and went into the bathroom. Terron knew he had him now. He slid in there after him. Fat Chop had just finish taking a piss. When he went to wash his hand he seen Terron come in.

"What's going on playa, you enjoying the show," he asked washing his hands with a big smile on his face. Fat Chop was what they called a social butterfly. He had to be in his line of work. He wanted everyone to come out and have a great experience. He tried to make it his business to speak to and get to know everybody, but at the moment he was trying to get to know the wrong person.

"Yeah, you did ya thing," Terron said. He knew that he couldn't let Fat Chop leave that bathroom. He walked behind him and put him in the dope fiend and drug him in the bathroom stall. Fat Chop was a big boy, but Terron was strong for his size. The shock is what took Fat Chop off of is feet. Terron held him tighter than a UFC fighter. Fat Chop was gasping for air. Then he closed his eyes and just let go. Terron held him for a few more seconds then let him drop. Thinking he straggled him to death he left the bathroom stall, locked it. Fixed himself in front of the mirror and was getting ready to leave when he heard a noise. He looked at the bottom of the stall only to see Fat Chop getting up. He pulled out his gun, kicked in the stall door and gave Fat Chop two to the head. He quickly got out of there hoping that nobody heard the shots.

"What took you so long," Suki asked?

"I was using the bathroom."

Terron seen a couple of Fat Chop security guards rush to the back.

"Come on, we're out of here," Terron said getting up and grabbing on Suki.

She knew something was wrong because she never seen him act how he was acting. She moved out with him no questions asked.

"Aye you," is what Terron and Suki heard as soon as they stepped outside of the building. "Freeze, put your hands up."

Terron's first instinct was to pull out, instead he took off running in his hard bottoms. He couldn't outrun them in them shoes. They hulked him down and found the murder weapon on him.

Kenyan watched the whole thing from the comfort of his car. He felt bad for his boy, he thought that he was about to get killed. They snatch Suki up but end up letting her go at the station. Turns out Fat Chop Security team was all DEA agents.

CHAPTER 13

The Courier Post Newspaper went into the long standing relationship that Fat Chop had with the DEA. This reporter had the scoop and was laying it all out there. Dudes In the city who had any type of dealing with him was in panic mode. Whoever was this reporter's source was even putting together scenarios of why Fat Chop had gotten killed. The feds must have had the same theory because they were drilling Terron for Answers.

"We know Kenyan got you to do it in revenge for his brother. Come on now, you think we don't know these things. All you have to do is say it, I promise you that we'll put you in witness protection," Lieutenant Lynch said.

Terron sat there calm as ever with his hands folded in his lap looking him in his eyes. Lieutenant had both hands on the table, a little bent over it staring, Terron in his eyes with the mean mug.

"Come on, tell me something," the Lieutenant said pounding on the table. Terron smirked at him causing his face to become Beet juice red. The other two agents who was in the room with them were mad also. It was apparent that they really wanted Kenyan, but Terron would never tell on his manz. Death before dishonor was an obligation that Terron felt should be held up by everyone.

"You think it's a game. It won't be funny when we send your ass up creak. At the end I'ma have the last laugh. I love my job and I'm going to get your boy."

Terron sat there through all the bullshit. They threatened him with everything, including an ass whooping. When it was all said and done, they turned him over to the state because they didn't have jurisdiction.

Even though the feds couldn't prove it, they knew that Kenyan had put the hit on Fat Chop. The prosecutor was also going hard at Kenny since they knew he was tied to them. Terron was given a two million dollar bail. In court the prosecutor tried to make Terron out to be this hit man for a well organized drug ring. He was making things up, throwing everything at Terron. Things that he knew nothing about was getting put on him, anything to paint him as a monster.

CHAPTER 14

Terron had just finished eating a hook up which consisted of two chicken soups, some Mackerel, with mayonnaise and some chips on the side. He sat on his bonk looking around his box of a cell at everything he owned, thinking to himself, *this ain't how it's supposed to be*. He had a 13-inch flatscreen Clear Tune TV. A big Panasonic radio that took tapes and CD's. People on the streets didn't use either anymore. He had a bunch of Islamic books on the shelf with his cosmetics. His food and clothes were under the bonk, and he had a little ice chest. That was basically everything to his name, jammed in one little room where he could touch both of the walls. No matter who you were or how much money a person was getting on the outside, everybody had the same things in prison. Some might have more, some less but it's all bullshit.

Terron had painted the floors and walls black reflecting how he felt on the inside. Only his shelves were green. When Terron was outside of his cell he was regular, but every time he entered that cell he entered a stage of depression. Only in his mind though, because he operated normal, but in that cell he always thought about how his people shitted on him. After all he did for dudes. He really thought dudes was his manz. The biggest disappointment was Kenyan, because he basically taught him everything he knew, but he didn't live up to any of it himself. He was the main one who left him there to rot.

No one told Terron about the fakeness in the game. He was finding out the hard way. Him and Kenyan was like brothers. At times they seemed closer than him and Kenny. So, for him not to show love at the darkest moments of his life was a hurt piece. Disloyalty was betrayal in Terron's eyes. These thoughts caused him plenty of sleepless nights. Dudes he used to deal with and who he would have probably done anything for, he now despised. He felt like they owed him everything, especially Kenyan since he was locked up for killing the person who told on his brother. He did it on the strength, he didn't even ask to get paid.

"Hello, put your mom on the phone Terron told his little cousin."

"Aunt Demi, I need you to do me a favor."

"What is it Nephew?"

"I need you to kick Suki out of my crib. She gotta go, she ain't playing her part. She can't be living for free no more. I could be renting that spot out, making money."

"Alright, you know I ain't never like her anyway. I might whop her ass if she acts up."

"Nah, I can't afford for you to get in trouble. I wrote her and told her that she had to pack her stuff and go. I need for you to enforce that. She probably got all kinds of dudes violating ma spot."

Their conversation was interrupted by a code going off in the prison. Once the code cleared Terron made his movement to the Law Library. He had to make a phone call to his Lawyer. His case was supposed to go in front a judge soon. While waiting to use the phone he was checking out all the clipping on the board. On the board there were newspaper clippings of laws, cases, people who came through that prison who left and ended up catching new charges and making the news. On there Terron saw a clipping of Kas and began reading the article. It had a picture of Kas shackled and handcuffed to the front walking in the courtroom looking sad. He had gotten fifty years for what he had did to that man in the mess hall.

****

"What was that code about earlier on y'all tier," Terron asked Quick?

"Nothing really, somebody sent the word from Northern State and dude got rolled out."

Terron nodded his head in approval. He liked and respected stuff like that. Whoever dude was that had gotten the other dude touched had long arms, that was power. He seen things like that happening, but it was always over something he considered weak, but in this case Quick had told him it was over some snitch stuff.

Terron had been thinking about everything that Quick was saying. After O'boy got touched, he knew that he could use that gang stuff to his advantage. He was in a powerless position and wasn't going anywhere. He figured if he could gain some power and take advantage of some people who were going home, then he could make some things happen on the outside, since his so called family and friends weren't coming through for him.

"I been thinking about what you was telling me bro. I might want in, but I'm not wit anybody putting their hands and feet on me."

"Nah, it ain't like that. Everybody don't get jumped in. I know you and ma word is good enough. What's up, you in?"

"I don't know, did you ever make ya mind up about what you was going to do?"

"Yeah, I'm dealing with ma manz and them who I showed you the pics of. He gave me double. Now I gotta build this thing up. I'm the only one under this over here on the east coast. This all us."

While they were talking this cool white boy walked up with a swag like he was black.

"What's good Terron?"

"What's up," Terron said back. Terron didn't really know him, but he seen him around talking to Quick. He knew that he was affiliated, but he didn't know if he was under the same banner as Quick. Quick was a power hungry person, so if he was in his ear then Terron knew that he was trying to get him under him if he haven't already. Since dude said Terron's name like he knew him Terron concluded that they must have talked about him.

"This ma guy Shoot First," Quick said introducing dude.

"Terron started laughing."

Quick did too. "Why you laughing? He thorough. He changed his name to be under me. He from Runnemede. He going to bring all the white clientele, plus you know I'ma be out there running through all the bunnies (white girls)," Quick said with a grin on his face.

"Why his name Shoot First?"

"Because he shoot first. That's the attribute I gave him. He gotta live up to that. Just like your attribute is Faruq. That means something that describes you, right?"

Faruq was Terron's Muslim name that only the brothers called him. The attribute the brothers took on were always positive, describing good characteristics or qualities that were seen in that brother. On the other hand, Terron knew plenty of dudes who was running around with these stupid killer names who wasn't living up to them. To him mostly every name he heard one of them dudes call themselves was corny. Still, he nodded his head and raised his eyebrows as to say whatever. He wasn't about to change his name.

Terron and Quick talked the whole yard period. By the end Terron was all the way in. He felt like fuck it, the way things were looking, he was never going home, and everybody fell off on him. All he could do was manipulate and take advantage of his surroundings. He didn't care anymore. He stopped Deening, going to Jumu'ah and Salaaming the brothers. One day one of the good brothers who he was fly with came to him trying to find out what was wrong.

"Faruq, you alright? I haven't been seeing you in the classes or in Jumu'ah. You know you can come and talk to me if you need to."

"I'm good, thanks though," Terron said being polite.

"Why haven't you been coming to Jumu'ah?"

"I haven't been feeling like it. It ain't in me no more."

The truth was that Terron had falling out of love with the Deen. He had got tired of the politics. Guys judging each other, talking behind dudes backs, saying that a brother is selfish when they don't get what they want, talking about they don't eat pork but smoking weed and sniffing dope. It was so much that he felt like he wasn't beat for anymore. When he was Deening he was taking it seriously. He was always on the front line while other dudes were playing with it.

The brother was a little blown away by Terron saying that it wasn't in him anymore. He believed that Terron was one of the brothers with deep faith, but he didn't know the struggle Terron had going on in the inside. The brother recited a couple of versus from the Holy Qur'an and some Hadiths, then tried to talk some sense into Terron but Terron was one of them dudes that when he made his mind up that was it. The Deen didn't move him how it used to. He had a new way of life. He was politicking with Quick heavy, trying to learn everything he could learn. Quick was giving him the history on everything and everybody, from the Black Panther Party to today, even on the dudes that was around them.

Being affiliated had its little benefits as far as prison goes, like Terron immediately got the plug with the weed and dope. He had automatic goons, but he stayed away from nut dudes. Being a natural leader, it didn't take long for him to gather his own pups. Quick gave him G under the set they were under.

"Whenever I move up, you move up with me. This our shit. Even when I go home, best believe I'm a keep in contact with you on the regular. I ain't none of these fake as dudes that forget about dudes, I got you. You going to have the inside and I'ma be making things happen from out there. You think we making moves now, wait until I get there. You not going to have to pay for nothing. It ain't going to be about nothing when I get there, real shit. I'ma make sure ya lawyer on his job and everything. I definitely need you out there with me."

Quick was about to go home soon so him and Terron was having some deep conversations about how things were going to be and how they were going to run things. Quick tried to think like a mobster in every expect. He wanted the inside of the prisons on smash, even when he went home. His set was new, but he knew that the bigger they got in prison the more power he'll have inside and outside of the walls. He seen and been around guys who had the type of power he was seeking, and he didn't feel like they deserved it, or even really knew what to do with it. He knew that they weren't half as thorough or smarter than him.

A few months later Quick went home. Terron had to run everything himself now. They only had about twelve dudes under them because they only dealt with thorough dudes with their minds right. Quick didn't want no nut dudes around, because that's why he left his last set.

Being the one in charge meant that all the problems the dudes under him had quickly became Terron's. There was always some internal problems going on amongst different sects of the sets. Quick had a reputation for putting in work so dudes already respected him, but Terron had yet to be tested.

Even though Terron had "G" he still had to beat the brakes off of a few dudes from different sets. He had to show them that he was like that. Dudes knew that he was given his status, nobody really respected that, so he was hearing things, and got tested, but every time he kicked up. The only way to get ya rep up in that life was to put in work. Every time he did, it added to his rep. He wasn't even a wild boy, but when he went in, he went in. Dudes eventually got the message that he wasn't to be messed with. Soon he became well respected, feared and even loved. Dudes started looking up to him and talking about him how they were talking about their big men.

Terron was in the cell in one of his darkest moments when he had got the bright idea to name himself Shaytan. The Arabic word for devil. He was serious, telling everybody not to call him Terron anymore. Dudes from Camden had stop messing with him. He didn't care. Every time somebody from Camden started gang banging, they were out casted. Most dudes from Camden was either Muslim or nothing.

Terron was in his cell looking at a Straight Stuntin magazine. He was reading the interviews. The one chick interview he was reading was looking good and she was talking salacious. He was thinking about jerking off to her. This dude from Camden came to his cell and called his name, "Terron."

Terron looked up with the mean face. "That ain't my name no more, it's Shaytan."

"Alright man, if you say so. Did you see the newspaper?"

"Nah."

"You in it, they said your case got over turned."

"I ain't hear nothing. I'll believe it when I see some paperwork or when these gates open up."

"I'ma try to get the paper for you. Dudes on the other side got it."

Dude left and came back with the newspaper in minutes. Terron sat there feeling all kinds of jitters as he read about himself in the paper. A half hour later two c.o.'s came and took him to lock up. They had to hold him there because he was no longer state property. Being in lock up didn't bother him now that he knew that it was true about his case. The next morning Camden County sheriffs came and got him. The state didn't drop the charges, but he was granted another trail. He was given a bail for a hundred and fifty thousand and posted bail the same night.

CHAPTER 15

Even Terron couldn't believe it, one minute he was sitting on forty five years to life, the next minute he was free. It didn't feel real to him yet. The first thing he did was hit this chick Toya house. He didn't give her a call or anything. She lived right down the street from his aunt's, so he just walked down there. He had on all black everything with a hood over his head as he walked down the street.

It took a few knocks, but when she opened the door and seen who it was, she became excited.

"O my god, when you come home," she asked hugging him?

"I been home," he lied while feeling her butt.

"Everybody was talking about you was never coming home."

"I know, I was hearing all the disrespect. Who here," Terron asked walking in her house.

"Just me and the kids."

"Ya kids?"

"No, I'm watching my cousin kids."

As soon as Terron went in the started pushing up on her for some pussy. It was no need to waste time. She knew what it was, the only time he ever showed up before when he was home was when he wanted some.

"Uhmm Terron, you're making me horny."

"Take these clothes off."

"I would but I'm on my period."

Terron had her against the wall with both hands holding her ass. When she said she was on her period he stopped nibbling on her neck, looked at her and asked," you not lying to me, right?"

"No, why would I lie? You know you can always get this."

"You got more holes than one," he said talking about her mouth, but she thought he was talking about ass.

"Boy what you been doing in prison," she asked looking at him funny?

"I'm talking about that throat action. I gotta put this thing somewhere," he said holding his man in his hand.

"I'll take care of that for you." She dropped to her knees and started going in. He treated her mouth like it was a pussy for about twenty minutes.

＊＊＊＊

After Terron got his nuts out of the sand he was able to see the world in its proper perspective again. Being deprived of pussy for so long could have a dude on sucka time, thinking that the world revolved around a woman and sex. That was only one expect of life.

He sat in his aunt's house evaluating his situation. The truth was that he didn't have a plan. He didn't have time to come up with one, everything happened so fast. He had Quick's information, he knew that he was going to eventually get up with him, but for the first time he was thinking about Kenyan. Unless they read the newspaper nobody really knew he was home. Hood people didn't read the paper like that. For that reason, he knew he could catch Kenyan slipping and do him dirty.

He smoked his Black & Mild while contemplating the situation. His feelings were mixed because he still had love for Kenyan, but Kenyan had left him for dead. His whole bid he was bitter over that. He knew that if he wouldn't have made it home then he would have never heard from him again. What made it so bad was that he always used to talk to Terron about principles, loyalty, don't snitch, death before dishonor, always be there for your friends, never bite the hand that feeds you, money over bitches and all this other supposed to be real stuff, but when it came down to it, he wasn't living what he was talking. Just thinking about it had Terron on edge. He couldn't let it ride, just off of principle. Something else Kenyan taught him.

****

Terron rode through the city in his aunt's car in observation. The city looked different from when he left. Camden was the core of Camden County. For a long time, it had been giving the county a black eye because it was the poorest and it was drug infested. They kept trying to revitalize it, building new buildings, knocking old ones down, paving roads, building parks but no matter what they did it still looked bad. There was always another abandon house, trash in the streets, and fiends roaming around like zombies.

Terron went out Parkside to the barbershop. When he walked in everyone was looking at him like this was back in the 60's and he was a black person walking in a white's only establishment.

"Terron," one of the barbers said trying to figure out if it was really him or not.

"What's good Spook?"

"Oh shit, what's up with you?"

Spook was an old dope head that use to cut Terron and his friends hair. He didn't have a shop, but he was so nice that no matter what shop he worked at, Terron and his dudes would go there. The last time Terron had seen him he was messed up with this young girl who he had turned out on dope. From the looks of things Terron figured he had gotten himself together and was doing good.

"You know, same old stuff. How many you got next?"

"I got you next. I just started him though. What's up with ya manz Kenyan, have you seen him yet?"

Everybody in the barbershop started paying Terron extra attention when Spook linked him to Kenyan. Dam near the whole city knew Kenyan. While Terron was gone he was out there doing his thing and was now one of the biggest drug dealers in the city.

At first Terron didn't know that spook worked at that barbershop. He went there because he didn't think any of his old friends would be going there but now that Spook was there, he knew they did go there. Terron knew that this was going to be his first and last time getting a cut there. The good news was that he found out that Kenyan go there.

CHAPTER 16

"Glad to see you home playa. I got something for you. I know you at least need the starter kit," Quick said.

"Yeah, I don't got shit right now. I still gotta fight that case. They ain't drop them charges, so you know I gotta get ma money up," Terron said.

"That's not a problem. I'm doing alright out here, still building this thing up though. Told you I was serious about this. Now that you're home, we're going to really make it happen. I got some young boys out East and some downtown. I be in Lindenwold too. These dudes are unconscious bro, they looking for a father figure so I'm sonning them," Quick said grinning. "I got all the connects, you got something you want to put together?"

"Tell you the truth bro, everything happened so fast for me that I didn't have time to put together a plan. I'm still kind of shocked that I'm home."

"Well you better put something together. You still have to fight that case. Alright, since you ma manz I'm going to give you a couple of my trappers so you can get on ya feet."

"That's what's up, but I can get my own trappers."

"Alright, but we in this together. I told you that I was going to bring you in. We building something here. You with me, right?"

"Of course, I'm with you all the way."

"Tomorrow I'ma introduce you to some of ma dudes. They not focused like us or where we at mentally but they ain't no clowns. You know I don't deal with them. I had to lower my standards a little when I got out here, everybody ain't leaders like us. That's not what you want from everybody anyway. These dudes follow orders and they thorough, that's what matter the most."

Terron didn't want to go back dealing with the same dudes that left him for dead. He didn't even want them to know that he was home, but he knew that they'll eventually find out. If he wanted to, he knew that he could easily get money with Kenyan, but he didn't think that he'll be able to hide his contempt for his disloyalty.

****

Terron pulled up to the crib out East. There was people hanging out front, everybody looked at him like he was in the wrong spot. Somebody must of told Quick that he was there because he came to the door. Terron didn't think anybody out there knew of him, but they did.

"Come in bro, let me show you around," Quick said. He was introducing Terron to everybody but when he told them Terron's name he didn't introduce him as

Terron he introduced him as Shaytan. Everyone he had got introduced to was acting like they were happy to have him be a part of their family. It was clear that Quick had been holding his name up because it was like they had heard of him.

"So, this Shaytan. It's good to meet you. Heard all good things about you bro. If you need anything let me know, I got you. This ma spot," Tec said.

"Thanks man." Dude was drunk but Terron could tell that his offer was genuine.

"That's Tec, he a canon, and he loyal," Quick said.

Terron nodded his head in approval. Getting together like this was what they did on the regular. Everybody just sitting around smoking, drinking, and mingling.

"You notice how it seem like some of them already know you" Quick asked?

"Yeah, I was thinking about that."

"That's because I made sure everybody close to me knew who you were. Some of the broads too. You'll be surprised how hard they go. We'll get to the business side of things tomorrow. Right now, enjoy yaself. I see some chicks checking you out. Go talk to them."

Quick left Terron standing in the Kitchen doorway looking around. He peeped him whisper something in some chick ear then he looked Terron's way as though he was talking about him. Afterwards the chick started walking towards Terron. Terron smirked as he checked her out. She was pair shaped down low. Up top she was a little smaller. Overall, her body was definitely right and Terron could tell that she knew it by the way she walked.

"Shaytan right," the chick asked as she took hold of Terron's hand?

"Yeah, what's up," he responded.

"Come with me," she said and began walking him through the crowd of people. Terron followed her upstairs into one of the rooms.

"Take ya clothes off," she commanded as if she was the dude.

Terron never had a chick talk to him like that. It almost made him laugh, but he just smirked and obeyed her order. She was extra thick, and he wanted to see what that was about. She came out of her clothes and his manz rose up in her direction like it smelt the pussy. She grabbed his dick and started rubbing it. She sat on the edge of the bed, and he stood there in front of her like superman as she pipped him.

CHAPTER 17

Kenyan pulled up to the barbershop in his White Bentley sitting on white twenty six inch rims. Dudes who was out front of the shop couldn't keep their eyes off of it. He walked right by only speaking to the dudes he knew on his way in the shop.

"I'm next right, Spook?"

Spook looked up from the tapper he was doing on the back of dude's head and said, "ma man." He stopped cutting his client's hair for a moment as him and Kenyan slapped hands and embraced. He had a lot of love and respect for Kenyan. Kenyan always looked out for him, even when he was doing bad. He never looked at him as a fiend.

"Let me finish him up, I got you."

Kenyan spoke to a few other dudes then started checking his phone.

"I seen ya boy T, he got big. I remember he was a stick figure."

"Who," Kenyan asked not sure who he was talking about? Terron was one of the farthest people from his mind.

"Terron, the skinny brown skin boy you used to be with. He caught that case back in the day that was all in the papers," Spook said trying to refresh his memory.

"Yeah yeah, I know who you talking about. You said you seen him, where at?"

"He came and got a cut a few days ago."

"You sure it was him? I think you mistaken, I ain't hear nothing about him being home," Kenyan said doubting Spook was talking about the right person. As far as he knew Terron still had Forty five years to life.

Everybody in the barbershop ears were open, being nosey. Even the guys that were talking was acting like they wasn't listening, but they were. Spook was surprised Kenyan didn't know that his manz was home. He remembered them being as tight as brothers.

"Nah, I'm telling you, he was in here. I cut his hair. I ain't lying to you. Aye Dirt, you remember dude Terron came in here right," Spook asked one of the other barbers? The other barber nodded his head yeah. "See, I'm telling you bro."

"Alright Spook," Kenyan said laughing at how excited he was getting. He was really trying to convince Kenyan.

"I ain't hear he was home but I'ma check him as soon as I leave here."

Kenyan still didn't really believe Spook saw Terron, but he was so adamant about it that he wondered could it have really been true. If so he questioned, then why didn't Terron come get with him.

****

Kenyan pulled up to Juice's condo. He got out of his car and noticed this lady looking his way. He didn't know if she was checking him out or his car. Then she smiled at him. He smirked and nodded his head a little but kept it moving. She was a good looking snow bunny. Franklinville was mainly all white, that's why Juiced moved out there.

"What's good," Juice said letting Kenyan in?

"You need to clean this thing up. You need a chick or something, you getting money, you can't be living like you broke," Kenyan said as he kicked Juice's clothes across the floor.

"Forget all that, this is how a bachelor's pad is supposed to look. You got some chicks you trying to bring over?"

"Nah."

"Well then, don't worry about ma cave. Where you going tonight? I see you got ya hair line tightened up. He chipped you too. You a little crooked."

"Yeah alright," Kenyan knew Spook didn't chip him. He didn't even have to look in the mirror after one of Spook's cuts, that's how confident he was in Spook's skills.

"I ain't going nowhere. Did you hear anything about Terron being home?"

"Nah, why?"

"Spook told me he came in the barbershop and got his haircut."

"He buggin, he might be sniffing that shit again."

"I don't think so, he sounded pretty sure. I'ma call Terron's aunt to find out if it's true."

"Hold up, let me get my stuff," Juice said before disappearing into the room.

CHAPTER 18

Terron walked through the dining room talking on the phone to some chick he had met at the mall the other day when he heard a knock at the door. Thinking it was for his aunt he opened the door without peeking through the peep whole first. To his surprise Kenyan and Juice stood there.

Terron was shocked but his face didn't show it. Hood dudes didn't react like regular humans. He had just smoked some weed, so his eyes were low and his face was plain.

"Dam fam, what you wasn't going to let nobody know that you was home? Let me get some love bro," Kenyan said with both of his hands up. Then he went in and shook Terron's hand and gave him a hug like he was happy to see him. Terron returned everything but with no enthusiasm. Kenyan didn't notice because he forced a bear hug.

"We miss you bro, now we can put the team together how it's supposed to be," Juice said.

"You already know, we out here getting money. How did you get home though, you won ya appeal?"

"I did, but it ain't over. I still have to go to court for it."

"Don't worry about that, we're going to get this money and have our lawyers knock that shit out of the park. Come on, let's go shopping. I know you need some stuff. We got a lot of catching up to do."

"Alright, hold up," Terron said and went back into the house to grab his sneakers and jacket. He was fully conscious of all the fake stuff. He just wasn't being ignorant while he was still trying to figure out how to play things. The wrong things said or done could turn into a beef. He took the hook up. It was on his mind how quick dudes would take their homie shopping when he came home but when he was behind the wall and needed stuff they didn't send him anything. The whole thing was ass backwards, because when dudes came home, they were able to get their own. That was all a part of the fakeness. Terron was some other type of dude, he despised everything fake. The love Kenyan and Juice was showing him he wasn't really beat for, of course they didn't know it though.

****

"Good looking for taking me shopping, that was some real shit," Terron lied.

"No doubt, it's only right, you bro. I'ma take you to drop them bags off and we going to go out tonight. Hit one of them strip joints over Philly. You know how we used to do," Kenyan said.

Kenyan seemed genuinely happy to have Terron back on the streets. He knew Terron was loyal, trustworthy, and dependable, but what he didn't know was how Terron really felt on the inside.

Kenyan took Terron to drop his stuff off and they went to the circle where everybody was at. Kenyan wanted to reintroduce him to his people. Terron got out of the car and was received by all kinds of looks from dudes he didn't know. Only a few dudes that was from out there was still out there. Everybody else was either dead or in jail or moved on in one way or another. Now it was a bunch of new dudes out there.

"This Terron I was telling y'all about," Juice said introducing him to everybody. Usually, dudes wouldn't be beat, but from what they heard about Terron they knew that he was somebody to be respected so they showed him the proper love and respect.

"As you can see the only thing that changed is the faces. I still got this thing on smash. We branched out to a few other spots. You know I always got a spot open for you. Whenever you ready let me know."

"What's up with Kenny," Terron asked Kenyan?

"They gave him twelve years for that charge. He alright though, I make sure of that. You don't be still messing with Suki, do you?"

"Nah, I been done with her."

"I warned you about her. She was out here letting dudes have their way with her. She used to be coming out here asking for money for you. We used to give it to her. After a while she was flirting with the trappers, next thing not one but a few of them was hitting it. Once I found that out, I stopped giving her money. I told the young boys that she was ya girl, but they didn't know you, so they didn't stop. She was smutting hard. She out here looking bad now though."

"Y'all was giving her money for me?"

"Yeah."

"She ain't send me nothing at all while I was down."

"All, she scandalous for that. Coming around here like she was collecting for you and keeping it. I didn't turn her down not one time. Wait until I see her."

Terron wasn't worried about her fucking. Any love he had for her was lost when he seen that she wasn't loyal. It pissed him off to find out that he wasn't getting the money that they were sending him. He started having second thoughts about how he should be feeling towards the dudes he thought shitted on him.

****

Ass was shaking everywhere in the club, but Terron wasn't excited. In prison his heart had become callous and cold from the lack of love. He seen everything different now. He looked at Kenyan and Juice throwing money on hoes. Nothing felt how it used to. He used to have fun doing things like that, but that was before he knew what things were really hitting for.

That night ended like many other nights did before Terron did his bid, with them taking a couple of strippers to a hotel and running through them. Stuff like that was the regular in the hood. It felt like he was going through the motions all over again. He couldn't believe that they were still out there doing the same thing.

Terron was getting coke from Quick and had a few dudes out East trapping for him. He also was getting coke from Kenyan and had got back in on the Circle. He kept everything separate and laid low. He wasn't playing the blocks how he used to, but he did his little pop ups here and there and chilled for a while. He didn't want Kenyan and them to know that he was a gang member. While he dealt with Quick heavy, he tried to keep his status on the low, mainly by not playing them other dudes too close. His bitterness would have to take a back seat because he was trying to get money. He wasn't going to forget how dudes left him for dead though.

CHAPTER 19

Terron heard the car horn honking, he grabbed his gun, jacket and left the house.

"What's good bro?"

"I'm good."

Quick passed Terron the Dutch. "We about to shoot up north to check big bro out."

"Who you talking about?"

"Hood, that's who I been dealing with. That's ma dude, I know you ain't see him in a while."

"I got ma gun on me, should I bring it?"

"Don't worry about it," Quick said pulling off. I got mine on me too. Even though we all homies, we can't forget that we still from Camden. A lot of dudes don't like us from up there."

"You right," Terron said. He leaned back in his seat and started smoking.

An hour and a half later they were in Newark New Jersey. "Yo bro, we out here. I'm on 16th Ave," Quick said. He was talking on the phone to Hood letting him know that they were on their way. Moments later they pulled up to this house. Hood was out there posted up with three other dudes. It was two motorcycles and a White Bentley truck in front of the house.

Quick pulled the Acura MDX over. They got out giving all of them dap. Terron could tell that Quick was used to going out there because of how comfortable he was and how fly he was with them.

"What's good with you," Hood said to Terron. They knew each other from doing time in Rahway together. Hood was one of the dudes they were buying dope off of. "When Quick told me you was home I couldn't believe it. That's a blessing, we need more dudes like you out here. What's good with you though?"

"I'm chilling. I see you doing it big though."

"This something light. Ma dudes stunt for a living. You'll see, y'all with me today. You don't have to worry about nothing."

Hood introduced Terron to the other dudes out there. They chilled out there and talked for a while longer as the night covered the sky.

Later that night Hood, Quick, Terron and Hood's manz Gauge jumped in the Bentley truck. The two other dudes jumped on their bikes and headed in the opposite direction.

"Here, taste this," Hood said passing Quick the Dutch.

Quick took two deep pulls and started gagging then coughing. When he stopped his eyes were watery.

"Dam, what's this," he asked looking at the Dutch while pounding on his chest?

"That's that gas," Hood said laughing.

"This serious, I gotta snatch up some of this to take back to the hood. They'll go crazy for this."

"I got you covered, don't even worry about it."

Terron got the Dutch and started gagging too. Hood pulled up on a bunch of dudes who was trapping in front of an abandon house. Everybody got out of the car, so Terron got out of the car too. He posted up on the car while Quick politicked with all the dudes from out there.

"Yo, this Terron, another one of ma CMD homies," Hood said.

"What's up with some of them Camden chicks," one of the dudes asked Terron while giving him a handshake?

"You don't want none of them," Terron said laughing.

"Shit if I don't. I know y'all got some official ones out there."

O boy introduced himself as Flame. Him and Terron started politicking. Dudes was out there serving fiends and pushing up on chicks that was walking by. A few dudes who were out there started a rap cypher. Terron was talking to Flame and some other dude, but he was on point, he was somewhere foreign. It was a lot going on out there. Terron peeped a cop car turn the corner and got a little nervous. The cop car slow rolled up to where everybody was, and everybody started going in different directions. Hood, Quick, Gauge, and Terron got in the Bentley and pulled off. The cop car started following them.

"Yo, we got it on us," Quick told Hood.

"Alright, I got you." Hood picked up the phone and called his dudes. "Yo, I got this cop on ma ass. Do something to get him off of me, I'm about to bring him around."

The cop was still following them. They turned the corner and seen a bunch of dudes on both sides of the street. The cops had put his police sirens on. As soon as he did that the dudes out there bombed his car with bricks and bottles. The cop stopped his car, Hood sped off treating the Bentley like a stolen car as he rocked each corner, slinging the ass of the car. Hood had the wheel. Terron knew he had to be out of that spot. He was in Newark getting chased by the cops and he was on bail. Hood rode to East Orange and pulled up to some crib. They got out of that car and jumped in a white four door 550 Benz. They started riding like nothing ever happened.

"Y'all stay strapped, that's why I fuck with y'all though, cause anything could happen out here," Hood said.

"We know that, we ain't trying to get caught slipping," Quick said.

"We going to this strip spot. Ma manz are going to be there. They might be there already."

****

From the outside they could tell that the spot was packed. It was people pulling up trying to find parking spots, some walking towards the club and a line to get in. It was on a strip full of warehouses. The Two dudes who were on the motorcycles earlier were now in front of the club waiting for them. They got out of the car and was walking pass this alleyway when they heard some smacking noises and moans. Their heads turned to see some dude smashing a chick from the back in the alleyway.

On the inside Terron was chilling. Every stripper who came over dancing on him he was trying to smash, that's how he was trying to enjoy himself. A lot of the fellas in there look like they weren't enjoying themselves. He seen a bunch of ice grills and sneaky looks. A lot of guys from out there had dreads and they kept their heads low with their dreads covering their faces, so it really looked like they were up to no good. Terron hoped that he wouldn't have to smoke any of them. He had been locked up with Newark dudes, he knew they always wanted rec when their crews were around. On the inside everything seemed cool though. They left after about an hour and a half.

At the end the club was letting out. Everybody was outside mingling trying to pull something to slid with when this black four door Impala came through with dudes hanging out of the windows. Terron saw them at the last minute. He didn't see any faces, but he did see a blue flag wrapped around the nose of what looked like an AK.

Shots rang out and everyone hit the ground. They were trying to hit everyone out there, males, females, it didn't matter. Their tires screeched as they sped off. Terron got off of the ground, pulled out his burner and let off about nine shots at the car. The car turned the corner and was gone.

****

"I'ma get with y'all. Terron, I hope you enjoyed ya day in Newark," Hood said laughing.

Terron smirked and said, "you gotta come to Camden sometime."

"I might take you up on that. Aye Quick, get with me when you ready."

"Alright bro," Quick responded.

Hood pulled off and Quick and Terron got in their car.

"You should drive. I'm tired and drunk," Quick said.

They switched sides and Terron drove back. Quick leaned his seat back and got comfortable so he could try to get some sleep on the ride back.

"We didn't even get any pussy. They like beefing more than they like getting pussy out that mothafucka."

"I got ma man played with a little. If I would of had a condom, I could have hit o'girl in there."

"It's alright, I could go without it. I ain't going to die," Quick said before duzzing off.

They got to Terron's house around 5:00 am. He woke Quick up. Quick got in the driver's seat and drove off.

****

Terron woke up around two in the afternoon. Still hung over, he got himself together and went to drop some work off to the block. He had yet to buy any wheels so that was on his to do list. He felt like he had way too much stuff to do to be walking or to be having to catch a ride from somebody.

"Let me use ya car Dev," Terron said to dude he had trapping for him.

Dev dug in his pocket, grabbed the keys and gave them to Terron without question. Terron made his way out East to go handle the rest of his business. Quick wasn't out there so he did what he had to do but didn't stay long. Even though he didn't really mess with them other dudes like that he didn't show it. They really respected him and his movements.

Terron dropped his money off home and took Dev back his car. He didn't mess with dudes from the circle like that either. That bid showed him what things were really hitting for. Now he was on some selfish, use everybody to get his, type of time.

"Kenyan said come around Mia's house," Dev told Terron when he got his car back.

Terron went around there to see what was up. Mia opened the door to let him in.

"Where you been," Kenyan asked?

"I was out of town. Why, what's up?" He didn't want to tell them who he was with or where.

"Nothing, just checking on you my guy."

You wasn't checking for me when I was locked up mothafucka, Terron thought to himself.

"I need you to take me to buy some wheels. Just something to get around in."

"I got you," Kenyan said taking a key off of his key chain. "That's to the Malibu. That's yours for as long as you want it or until you cop something new."

Kenyan took Terron to the car. Usually, Terron would want his own but since he was still kind of fresh out, he settled for the hand me down. He wasn't really trying to spend his money anyway.

Terron was sitting in the car with the door open cleaning it out, making sure wasn't any drugs in there that somebody forgot. He knew how unconscious dudes were. He was looking in the middle console when this chick walked by. She looked in the car, he looked up and they caught eye contact. She gave him a little smirk that told him all he needed to know.

"Hold up baby girl, you got a name," he asked getting out of the car?

"Nadia," she said.

"Nadia," Terron repeated nodding his head. "I like that. Terron. You should let me take you out sometimes Nadia."

"I'm sorry, but I'm in a relationship."

"Yeah, are you happy?"

"It could be better," she responded.

"You know I never understood why women stay in relationships when they're not happy."

"It's called being in love."

"Well, you should be in love with somebody who makes you happy. Here let me give you something." Terron went to his car, got a piece of paper, wrote his number down and gave it to her. "Just hold on to it, you might want to be happy one day. When you do, call me." He walked off. She was looking at the paper. When he turned around again, she was logging the number in her phone. He knew that he'll be hearing from her.

Now that Terron had some wheels he was able to move around and handle his business more efficiently. The next morning he went to go see his lawyer.

"Hello, how may I help you," the secretary asked as he entered the room. She didn't know who he was because this was her first time seeing him.

"Mr. Walls, I have an appointment with Mr. Rosenhower."

The secretary began looking at her computer, then she picked up the phone and told Mr. Rosenhower that a Mr. Walls was here to see him. He told her to let him in.

"How are you doing today Mr. Walls?"

"I'm making it, just trying to find out what's the latest with my case."

"Well, it's really too early right now. The prosecutor will probably wait a while, then come with some kind of plea bargain. Nine times out of ten it's going to be outrageous, and I'll tell him to shove it. As soon as I hear something you'll hear something. Your number is still the same, right?"

"No, that was my aunt's number."

"Alright, what is yours," Mr. Rosenhower asked grabbing a pen a pad. Terron gave him his number and left. He knew he had to stay on his lawyer, this was his life in the balance. He wasn't trying to go back and continue doing a life sentence. Since he was the lawyer who got Terron's sentenced overturned, he kind of trusted the way he did things.

****

Terron rode through Randolph Street where he happened to see Quick out there talking to a white dude. He thought that it might have been vice or something but upon a closer look he recognized the face and pulled over.

"Shoot First, what's up playa?"

"O shit, what's up bro," Shoot First said holding his hands up.

It was rare for a white boy to be posted up in the hood how he was. Everybody on the block was checking him out. The way Quick and Terron embraced him was like a stamp of approval. It caused everyone who was watching to see him in a different light.

"When you get out," Terron asked?

"Yesterday," Shoot First answered.

"This thing about to really come together," Quick said.

"I'm ready to make it happen, just let me know how and we're we going to do this," Shot First said rubbing his hands together. He was a thorough dude, but one could hear the suburbs in his voice.

They were standing there on the sidewalk talking when they heard a horn beeping. Terron turned around and seen Kenyan stopped in the middle of the street looking at them. He started walking over to the car.

"You alright out here," Kenyan asked? Kenyan knew that they were gang banging out there. When he seen his manz there he wanted to make sure he was good.

"Yeah, just talking to a couple dudes I was locked up with," Terron said.

"You rock with these dudes like that?"

Terron looked at him without giving him an answer. He knew why he asked him that, but only if he knew what was going through Terron's mind.

"Just be safe out here. You know they be on some nut shit."

"I hear you," Terron said at the same time thinking, *get the hell outta here*. He wasn't beat for anything. To him all these dudes were the same and he was going to treat them the same and use them all.

Since Shoot First was fresh out Quick wanted to get him some, so he took him to these bird's house on 29th Street. They were all smuts, but none of them ever let a white boy smash before.

"Who him," Sierra asked walking up to Shoot First? "He cute, come on," she said taking him upstairs to give him his first piece of black pussy. He got turned out and after that all he wanted was black chicks.

Shoot First opened another world to Quick and Terron. He took them out Runnemede and introduced them to a different clientele. All white people that had good jobs and families. The type of people who most people wouldn't guest was doing drugs. Powder was mainly their drug of choice. Terron and Quick was able to charge them double the regular price. They were doing their thing out there. In Runnemede everyone called Shoot First Timothy. He became real popular amongst the crowds out there because he had connections to get whatever kind of drug they wanted. He would get invited to parties and raves and sometimes Terron and Quick would join him. He even put some parties together himself.

CHAPTER 20

Six months on the streets flew by. The prosecutor offered Terron 25 years with 85%. He told his lawyer to tell the prosecutor to suck his dick, he's not taking it. Of course, the lawyer didn't decline the offer in that manner, but he did let him know his client wasn't willing to take any high numbers. For the prosecutor that meant time, money, and energy, but he acted like he was going to play hard ball. That was the art of the deal. It was a real life poker game, but the way Terron was feeling, if they kept talking like that then he wasn't going to go in at all. He was making money, so he was just going to be out.

****

"I just seen Terron out East. He been dealing with them dudes a lot, you think he into that stuff," Juice asked?

The way Terron moved didn't reveal that he had any affiliations to that. He didn't wear any one color heavy or wear bandannas or talk their slang. Only the dudes he dealt with that was on it knew what he dealt with.

"Nah, I think he just got something out there. He getting a lot of money messing with them dudes, so I ain't mad at him," Kenyan said.

With everything that Terron had going on he started buying more coke off of Kenyan, that's how Kenyan knew he was getting more money. That was only about half of what he was really doing because Terron and Quick still had their Newark connect.

Even though Terron was getting money he wasn't trying to shine or anything. He was staying low and trying to stack as much money as he could before he had to go in and finish whatever time he took, if he was going to take any time at all.

Terron walked out of the store just in time to bump into Nadia. She was with some other chick. Terron didn't pay the other chick any mind.

"What's good Nadia," Terron said putting his arm around her shoulder as he walked with them. "I see you never used that number I gave you. You must not be ready to be happy yet. You still messing with the same dude?"

The girl that was with her pushed Terron's arm off of Nadia's shoulder and said, "excuse you." At the same time looked at Terron like she wanted to go some rounds.

"You alright," Terron asked confused"

"Are you alright," The chick asked and threw her arm around Nadia, taking her away from him.

"Oh shit, ma bad," Terron said smirking. He eventually got the picture. He didn't know why he didn't catch it in the first place. The other chick was short stubby with a short haircut and wore her clothes like a dude. She even had a dude swag. It was only one thing, she wasn't a dude. Terron couldn't understand why a chick would be in a relationship with a chick that's trying to look and act like a guy, when the whole idea of being with a woman was because she liked women. He didn't feel any type of way at how she shoved his arm. He laughed it off and respected their relationship. He turned around and seen Juice and Butter laughing at him.

"That ain't no man, I don't know what the fuck that was. It was tough as hell though."

"That's Big Roxy. She used to trap out here with us while you were gone. She did a bid and fell back when she came home," Butter said.

"She probably was raping chicks while she was down. You seen how she push ma arm?"

"All man, you let her push you. He let Big Roxy chump him," Juice told Butter laughing.

"You can't soup me up, I know what I'm capable of."

Dudes stayed souping people up in the hood for laughs and entertainment. Terron was a vet though, he wasn't beat. He had pass that stage in life. Now everybody was entertainment for him, rather they knew it or not. He didn't even like laughing and joking with them dudes how he used too. People who knew him noticed a big change in his attitude and the way he moved. Most of them chalked it up as him being in prison. They knew prison could cause some dudes to grow up, they also knew it messed a lot of dudes up.

Kenyan saw Terron as being more focused. Besides him dealing with some weirdos he was getting more money. That's all that really mattered. Terron never showed Kenyan nothing but love so it was all love, so he thought.

CHAPTER 21

"I seen ya manz the other day, what's up with him," Raheem asked?

"He good. You know right back to it. I'm about to go meet up with him as soon as I leave here."

"I been seeing him keeping some bad company. Around dudes who be gang banging, all they do is make shit hot."

"I feel what you saying. I don't want him around them dudes either, but he grown. I don't think he on that type of time, he just caking off from them dudes," Kenyan said.

"I heard that he one of their top men."

"Yeah, you serious?"

Raheem nodded his head yeah. Kenyan knew if Raheem heard it then more than likely it had some truth to it.

"I'ma talk to him and find out, because I really want to know," Kenyan said before leaving.

****

Kenyan and Butter got out of the GMC truck. Butter was in the back seat grabbing the bags. Kenyan had just shut the driver's door when four mask men ran up on them. Kenyan seen them, pulled out his burner and popped one dude. At the same time dude shot him in the stomach, buckling him to the ground.

Shots started ringing out. Butter got bodied from the door. As soon as the dudes that was heading for him heard the first shot, they lit Butter up. Kenyan and other dudes were still banging at each other. The first dude Kenyan shot in the chest was on the ground squirming. Kenyan began trying to get up, but he couldn't. He tried dragging himself towards the house. He hoped that Terron and Juice heard the shots and would come out blasting.

When Terron and Juice first heard the shots, they looked at each other, got up and got their guns. Terron ran to the window to see the action. Juice didn't bother, if something was going down with his manz he was riding. He grabbed the doorknob to open the door but before he could get it open all the way he heard Terron's gun cock, then felt the cold piece of steel pressing against the back of his head.

"What you doing?"

"What you think I'm doing? Close that door," Terron said taking the gun out of Juice's hand.

Kenyan was still shooting at the other side when he heard a click. The other dudes were hiding behind cars. The click seemed so loud to Kenyan that he thought they heard it. He started panicking thinking he was fucked. He looked back at the house just in time to see the door closing. He wondered, *why it was closing instead of opening? Why wasn't his dudes shooting him any bail.* He started to panic checking his gun to see if he had any bullets left, which he already knew it didn't, but he was desperate.

While Kenyan was praying for God to send down an extra clip three mask men came from behind a car in all black looking like ninjas. They stood over top of him and together shot him about ten more times.

Terron still had his gun to Juice's head, at the same time he kept looking through the blinds to see what was happening. He seen two dudes get into Kenyan's truck and the other dude ran back to his car.

Juice was scared to death. He figured that Terron had set Kenyan up because they were sitting there waiting for him to come back with the coke.

"We supposed to be family. I can't believe you doing me like this."

"Family, mothafucka you ain't ma family. Where was my family when I was doing forty five years to life."

"I'm saying though."

"You ain't saying nothing, shut the fuck up and face the wall," Terron said poking him real hard twice in the back of the head. He had him facing the corner of the wall near the door. Juice shut up like he was told in hopes that Terron would let him out of there alive. The Terron he knew wasn't a cold blooded killer. In fact, other than the time he killed dude for Kenyan he never knew Terron for bussing his gun at all, so he figured the percentage of him living was high. The one thing he didn't know was that before doing that situation for Kenyan, him and Kenyan had bodied them dudes from downtown. Terron was more devious than Juice thought. The numbers really weren't in his favor like he thought.

Terron pulled out his phone and called Quick

"Yo, everything good?"

"Yeah yeah, get out of there."

"Alright, on ma way."

BOOM BOOM!

He shot Juice twice in the back of the head, opened the door and left. The block was still quiet and dark. Terron went and stood near Kenyan. It looked like Kenyan was staring up at him. Terron could tell that he was fighting for his life. His eyes had got low then he opened them back up. His body wasn't showing any movement. With the intentions on making him feel the hurt that he felt when he was in them cells Terron shot him one last time and mumbled, "you disloyal mothafucka."

People who lived on the block didn't come out of their houses until the police showed up. They didn't want to witness anything because they didn't want anybody coming back for them. The cops found two men on the sidewalk. They assumed they were both dead until one of the cops got close enough to Kenyan and seen that he was still alive. "We got a breather!" They began working on him and rushed him off to the hospital. The neighbor told the police that him and his wife heard shots coming from next door, so the police went in there and found Juice's body.

The Doctors manage to save Kenyan's life, but he was in critical condition. All though he survived twelve shots, the Doctor told his family that they didn't know if he would ever be the same.

****

Terron and Quick took the majority of the bricks but they rewarded their soldiers handsomely for a job well done.

"This shit right here go to the grave with us no matter what," Terron said telling his dudes something Kenyan had taught him years ago. "If they weren't here then it's no need for them to know. In fact, if any of us ever bring It up again don't trust him, he's working with them boys. It's no need for us to ever talk about this again."

Everybody there was nodding their heads, even Quick. He knew that was some real stuff Terron was talking.

The police found Kenyan's truck engulfed in flames in Centerville on Masters Street near the railroad tracks. They didn't connect it to the murders though.

CHAPTER 22

The next day Raheem got word about what happened to Kenyan. He knew that it had to be a robbery because he had just served him the mother load. He also figured that it had to be someone he knew. Who else would know that he was making a move? He had loss some money in that deal. He told himself that he was going to get to the bottom of things.

Over the years Kenyan had become a part of something bigger. He was well connected with the brothers, and since he was one of them, Raheem wasn't going to let what happened to him go unanswered.

Raheem pulled up on Terron talking to "Z" in the circle.

"You said he still alive," Terron asked shocked?

"That's what his mom said. She said he in real bad condition though. He in a comma. I'm going up there tomorrow, you coming," Z asked?

"Nah, I'm a wait until he wakes up. I'm definitely going to pay bro a visit though," Terron said thinking if only Z knew what kind of visit he was talking about. Kenyan was stronger than Terron thought. When he seen him that night, he looked like he was about to walk into that white light. He regretted not giving him a face shot.

Raheem called Terron to the car. Terron remembered him from back in the day, he knew that's who Kenyan was dealing with. He walked to the passenger side window.

"What happened with Kenyan last night?"

"I don't know. I'm just finding out myself. My manz about to go check him out in the hospital."

"You mean he still alive," Raheem asked?

"Yeah, that's what I heard. They're saying that he's in critical though."

While Terron was talking something had dawned on Raheem. Terron said that he had just found out what happened to Kenyan, but he remembered when him and Kenyan was talking last night about Terron, Kenyan said something about Terron was waiting at the spot for him. Something smelt fishy to Raheem.

"So, when are you going to go see bro?"

"I don't know. I'm surprised they're letting him get visits. One minute they're saying he in a comma, next minute they're saying that he in critical condition. I might just wait a few days."

Raheem knew bullshit when he smelt it. He just wanted to look in Terron's eyes to see for himself if he had anything to do with it or not. He was almost certain that he did.

****

When Terron told Quick that Kenyan was still alive, Quick couldn't believe it.

"I shot that fool at least three times in the chest," Quick said.

"They said he holding on for dear life in there. I was thinking about paying him a visit. I fuck around and pull that plug," Terron joked.

"You playing, we might really have to get at him," Quick said.

"I'm saying, I ain't doing nothing to him in there, we can send the goons though."

"That's what the goons are for. They already dead, they just waiting to be sent on that suicide mission."

"You serious, huh?"

"You dam right I am," Quick responded.

"Alright, let me pay him a visit first."

Terron went to visit him on a Friday night. He figured wouldn't nobody be there then. The hospital was quiet, so much so that Terron could hear his own footsteps while walking down the hall. The lights were dim, all the better for Terron because he didn't want anyone knowing that he was visiting Kenyan. He used Kenyan's brother Kenny's name to get in.

Terron walked in the room and seen two dudes laying sound asleep in their hospital beds. He walked up to one of them and seen that it was Kenyan. He looked around and shut the curtains that separated Kenyan from the other dude in the room. Kenyan was hooked to a machine, which was helping keep him alive. The thought of pulling the plug crossed Terron's mind, but he wasn't that stupid. He canceled that thought. He held both hands behind his back as he looked Kenyan over. He didn't like the fact that it had to go down like it did. He sat in the chair by the bed and chilled for a few seconds.

"Kenyan, I know you can still hear me. They say people in commas can still hear shit, so I know that you know I'm here. I wish that it didn't have to go down like this. I mean, you was ma bro. I would of did anything for you. You was ma brother. I really looked up to you, you just don't know. You taught me everything I know as far as how to get money and put in work. You taught me about loyalty, then didn't show me any. I had life bro, you left me for dead. Where is the loyalty in that? You ain't practice nothing you preached."

Thinking about his days in prison was making Terron upset. How he had them letters on his back suffering mentally, not knowing if he was ever going to see the streets again. The whole time sitting there he was looking at Kenyan.

"You ain't real, you a fraud. Don't nobody knows it but me. You selfish and don't care about anybody but yaself. I don't care what anybody else think about you, I know you. I got ya card. You know I do."

Terron stood up and looked down on Kenyan. He spoke in a low tone. While talking he seen Kenyan's fist clench. Terron smiled as he seen it get tighter.

"See, I knew you could hear me. I hope you enjoyed this visit because it's going to be ya last one. See you on the other side pussy. (Chhaagh tah)." Terron filled his mouth with a big glob of hulk spit and slimed kenyan's face with it.

Kenyan laid there with what looked like slime oozing down his face. No facial expression to show how he was feeling on the inside.

"You can unclench ya fist, you can't do shit," Terron said. Afterwards he left feeling better than when he arrived.

CHAPTER 23

A few days later Kenyan's mother, girl and two daughters were in his room visiting him when two police officers came in and slapped some handcuffs on him.

"What's going on officer," his mother asked?

"His fingerprints were found on a gun that was on a murder scene."

Kenyan's family was devastated, it was nothing that they could do. The cops let them continue with their visit, but one cop was to remain in that room with Kenyan at all times.

While Kenyan was in the hospital suffering Terron was in the hood balling the same way Kenyan was when he was locked up. He took over the circle and kept everything moving. Nobody suspected anything.

Three weeks after Terron had visited Kenyan he sent two of his dudes to finish him off for good. They had no problem getting pass the desk and making it upstairs. The hospital was so busy that they basically went unnoticed. Terron had told them his room number but once they got up their it was a police officer in there. He sat in a chair dozing off. They slid into another room to try to come up with another way to get to Kenyan without the cop catching them.

"We can just wait for him to go to sleep and walk right by him."

"Man, I ain't trying to be here all night. I gotta take one of them nervous shits right now."

"You scary as hell, always nervous."

"I just want to get this over with. If I was scary, I wouldn't be here."

"You want to body the cop too."

"Nah, it gotta be a better way."

"Alright look, I'll distract him, getting him away from the room, you slide in there and do what you gotta do."

"Nah, how about I distract him, and you slide in there and do what you gotta do."

"It don't matter, we here for the same purpose."

One of the dudes went out the room and approached a nurse.

"Excuse me nurse, where is my brother? I need to know where my brother is at. I was told that he was up here."

He was acting hysterical. The little white lady was afraid.

"Sir, what are you doing here? It's not visiting hours. You can't see your brother right now. You have to come back tomorrow."

"What the hell you mean come back tomorrow. I want to see my brother now," Dude said getting loud. The cop was awakened by how loud he was. He looked down the hall and seen that there was a problem, so he got up and started walking towards them. As a police officer it wasn't uncommon to run into a drunk or a crazy person that was acting a fool. He had already diagnosed this as one of those cases.

When the cop left the room, the other hit man slid right in. He seen Kenyan laying there knocked out and handcuffed to the bed. He went over to his machine and started unplugging everything. Eventually Kenyan stopped breathing and flat lined. When he flat lined the machine made a loud steady beep. The nurses who were with the cop trying to get the hitman who was distracting them out of the hospital heard it and took off running down the hall towards the room. The first nurse got to the entrance of the door and was startled by the hitman leaving. He quickly brushed by her and started walking in the opposite direction of the cop. It didn't take but a second for the nurse to figure out what had just happened.

"Officer officer," she yelled at the top of her lungs pointing at the bad guy as he took off running.

The cop seen her pointing and dude running, he immediately took chase. The hitman who was the distraction quietly walked off. The nurse in the room had quickly plugged all the machines back up, but it was too late. She also tried CPR, but nothing worked.

On his way out of the hospital the hitman who was the distraction pulled the fire alarm causing mass chaos in the hospital. People were scrambling which helped the other dude get away from the cop who was on his heels.

Before what happened to Kenyan had hit the hood, the streets were already talking about how they felt like Terron had did something grimy. He never grieved. Instead, he began splurging and making his affiliations known.

Terron didn't care about what the streets was talking. None of them was riding with him when he had life. He was on the block talking to his manz Cruz when Shoot First pulled up. Everybody in the circle was looking at him like he was Vice until Terron acknowledged him.

"What's good ma nig," Shoot First said as he gave Terron dap, and they embraced?

Cruz heard the whiteboy say the N-word and was looking at Terron thinking how you let him get that off.

What he didn't know was that Shoot First was his manz and that he was going to ride with him before any of them dudes out there.

"Cruz, this ma manz Shoot First, Shoot First this is Cruz." Terron didn't even introduce Cruz as his manz, making a clear distinction.

Shoot First and Cruz gave each other dap, then Shoot First and Terron began talking. Dudes on the block was checking Shoot First out. He was dressed in red from head to toe. Dudes knew what it was. Even though they weren't feeling it, they weren't thinking about doing anything about it. Terron started trying to put them on what was about to go down, but they acted like they didn't want to convert, so he began bringing dudes from out East to the circle. He figured that eventually they'll get down with the movement or get moved out. Either way he didn't care as long as they stayed in pocket.

Chapter 24

Raheem felt bad for Kenyan when he found out what had happened to him at the hospital. The papers were talking like it was a professional hit. It was all over the news. The nurses told their sides of the story to the news channels. The Police Commissioner had a press conference. They knew a lawsuit was coming. The two dudes were caught on camera throughout the hospital.

While the Police Commissioner was giving his press conference there was two big pictures of the assassins on a stand up billboard right next to the commissioner with the letters wanted written in big bold red letters. The news stations kept zooming in on their faces. It was also a twenty thousand dollar reward for any information that led to their arrest.

The city was on fire. They really wanted these guys. The murder was too brazen to go unsolved. Camden police was getting pressured, which meant they had to put more pressure on the streets, which meant dudes couldn't get money how they wanted so a lot of dry snitching started happening. Nobody really knew exactly what was going on but Quick's and Terron's name kept popping up.

"Yo man, what we going to do? They got our faces everywhere," Wildout said.

"Calm down, let me think," Gunplay said sitting on the couch holding his head, looking at the floor.

Wildout was too nervous to stay still. He kept pacing the floor smoking Black and Mild's. He was pulling on the Black and Mild so hard it was sinking in looking like veins.

"You know what, we going to call these mothafuckas, they gotta get us out of here. At least as far away from Jersey as possible."

"You're right, go ahead, call them."

****

"Hello," Quick answered his phone?

"It's Gunplay."

"What's up with y'all, where y'all at? These mothafucka out here turning shit upside down and inside out looking for y'all."

"I know man, we're fucked. What are we going to do? We gotta get out of here."

"I got you, don't even worry about it. Where y'all at?"

Quick told Gunplay that they were going to come get them around midnight. When he hung up the phone Terron was sitting there looking at him.

"You know we have to get rid of them, right?"

"Rid of them like what," Quick asked?

"It's over for them. They're going to get caught rather it's ten years from now or twenty, we gotta tie up any loose ends, so that shit can't get back to us. I ain't trying to take any chances."

Quick knew where he was getting at, but he still was thinking about it. He had grew up with Gunplay and Wildout. They had been loyal to him. On the other hand, Terron didn't care about either one of them.

"I'm telling you bro, you'll be surprised what dudes a do when their trying to get out of a jam. Ain't nothing funny about having life, you know I been there. I still got dark spots under ma eyes from stressing. I know they're ya dudes but they kind of botched the mission. They were supposed to handle things quietly. Get in and out without anybody seeing them."

"You right," Quick reluctantly agreed.

Terron had successfully convinced him. As soon as Terron seen that they were caught on video he knew if he was to get to them before they got locked up then he would have to dead them with or without Quick.

****

Terron and Quick pulled up to the house Gunplay and Wildout was at. They came running out to the van with their hoodies on their heads.

"Who live there," Quick asked as Terron pulled off?

"Some fiend chick," Gunplay answered.

"A fiend, I'm Surprised she didn't turn y'all in. I was watching the news earlier and they up that rewards money to fifty thousand."

"She don't know what's going on in the real world. I don't even think it was a tv in that mothafucka," Gunplay said.

"We're going to get y'all down south. To Florida, but not today. Right now, we just going to get y'all out of the state. Tomorrow we're going to take that ride.

"I know y'all trying to smoke some of this," Quick said passing Wildout the Dutch.

They had smoked two Dutches before Terron pulled over in Fairmont Park in Philly. Gunplay and Wildout was so laid back that they weren't even paying attention to where they were. Once the van stopped a masked man slid the van door open shocking both of them. They seen the AK 47 pointed at them and started trying to climb over one another to get out of the way of them bullets.

"O shit, Quick man," was the last thing Terron and Quick heard before they got out of the van. Terron ran to the other car and grabbed the gas can. After dude hit them up with the AK, they lit the van on fired and left.

CHAPTER 25

"So, you think his manz had something to do with it," Anwar asked?

"I'm almost sure Sheik. I remember he told me that he was about to go meet him. All of a sudden he gets hit up and robbed. I pulled up on dude and he acted like he didn't know nothing when I know for a fact Kenyan was going to meet up with him after he copped. Kenyan didn't even know he was gang banging. I had said something to Kenyan about who his manz be dealing with, but he doubted it. All of a sudden, he wide open with it. I had got the word that the two dudes that's on the run is his peoples."

Anwar turned down the corner of his mouth and nodded his head acknowledging that everything did make sense.

"Alright."

"Alright what," Raheem asked?

"Do you really need me to say it?"

"Nah, not really."

The Sheik was nonchalant about everything. One had to be around him to know how he was. He was such a vet that he rarely said anything that would incriminate himself, so Raheem had to know what he was saying without him saying it.

****

Shoot First had a regular house party at his house in Runnemede. Quick and Terron were the only dudes from Camden in there. Shoot First wasn't stupid, he knew he couldn't invite too many dudes from the hood to the suburbs and expect nothing to happen. It was other black people there, but they were from the suburbs. Terron and Quick had just gotten to know them since Shoot First came home, or Timothy rather because that's what they called him out there. They knew Terron as Shaytan.

It was bunnies everywhere in there. Everybody was on some type of drug. Mushrooms, E-pills, coke, weed, powder etc…. The white boys were over in one area holding each other upside down drinking beer out of a cag. The music was playing all hip hop and pop. When that song (I kissed a girl and I liked it) came on, a few bunnies started kissing one another. Terron went around socializing, all the ladies were on him. The dudes were a little rowdy, but not wild. They respected Shoot First things. It was the opposite feeling dudes had when they were in the hood. Terron eventually found two bunnies who he took upstairs and had a threesome with.

****

Camden County Police was in cohorts with the DEA and the state police to crack down on Camden's crime, especially all the murders that was happening. Lieutenant Lynch was heading the DEA division. He was seated at his desk when he received a phone call from the Philadelphia homicide division telling him that two guys from Camden was found murdered and burnt beyond recognition. When he told Lieutenant Lynch their names, he became livid.

"Fuck," he blurted out! Excuse me. Them guys were wanted over here for a murder. We really wanted them. When Lieutenant Lynch had his meeting, him and his team followed their leads which lead them to Terron and Quick. He did his homework on them both and found out that he remembered Terron.

"This guy used to be one of Kenyan Perkins main guys. Why would he want him dead," Lieutenant Lynch asked himself, trying to figure things out? He said it loud enough for everyone else that was sitting in the room could hear.

"Maybe they had a falling out or something," the lady agent said.

"Alright, let's see, what do we know about this guy. First let's put everything into perspective. Back in the day we had a snitch name Scott working for us. He helped us lock Kenyan's brother up, Kenny Perkins. We caught him with some cocaine. Who we really wanted was his brother Kenyan. We always knew he controlled things. When our snitch got killed, we caught Terron red handed at the scene. He still went to trial, and he ended up getting forty five years to life."

"How did he get out of prison," the lady agent blurted out?

One of the other agents, Agent John shot her a mean look letting her know to shut up and listen.

Lieutenant Lynch continued. "He got back on an appeal and bailed out of the county. He's still facing them charges. Let me get back to what I was saying. When we caught him, I questioned him myself because I knew that Kenyan had sent him to do it, but he kept his mouth shut. He's definitely one of them hardcore guys. My thing is all these leads are leading up to him having something to do with Kenyan Perkins death. Then what's his motive, and how was this guy connected," Lieutenant Lynch asked pointing to Quick's picture. "These are things that we have to find out."

CHAPTER 26

Terron appeared in court looking like money. He had a three piece Taylor made Armani suit on and a pair of Ray Band glasses with no prescriptions in them. He just wore them so he could look preppy. He watched frustrated as his lawyer and the prosecutor went back and forth. He wondered why was the prosecutor going that hard at him, it was only a hearing he thought to himself. He kept catching the judge eyeing him down, but he couldn't tell what that look was about.

Lieutenant Lynch was seated in the back of the courtroom with another agent listening to everything. He already had a long discussion with the prosecutor. That's one reason why the prosecutor was going so hard at him. Before they went into the courtroom Terron's lawyer had his own talk with the prosecutor to see what kind of deal could be worked out, but the prosecutor had only offered to take the life off of his original sentence.

That day in court messed Terron's whole day up. He was hoping they would offer him something he could work with. Maybe a 12 with an 85%. He had half of that in and it would have had been nothing for him to finish that up since he would get time served. At first his lawyer had him optimistic, thinking it was a possibility that he could get time served, but when he came back with what the prosecutor said he started thinking about firing him.

Terron walked outside of the courthouse. Lieutenant Lynch and agent John started walking along each side of him.

"So, we meet again," Lieutenant Lynch said. "How are you enjoying your freedom?"

Terron looked at both of them with his hands still in his pockets, "What I do now?"

"So far, I can't prove you did anything, I'm still working on that. Do you feel like coming to the station to answer some questions?"

"Do I really have a choice?"

"See, I commend you for that. Who said guys don't get smarter when they go to prison," Lieutenant Lynch said laying his hand on Terron's back guiding him towards his unmarked car.

Terron shrugged his shoulder back to get his hand off of him.

****

At the station they went through the same routine they did when they first met before, but this time the Lieutenant really didn't have anything on him.

"Where were you January 16th?"

"How am I supposed to remember? That was months ago, I don't be keeping track of the dates"

"OK, no alibi. How about February 28th, where were you then?"

Terron looked at him, "What's up with these dates? Why you wonna know what I was doing on these date?"

Terron already knew the reason why he was asking the questions he was asking. He just was playing the stupid role.

"You know I can't figure out why would you kill your friend Kenyan?"

"What, I don't even know who that is."

"O so you don't know him now." The Lieutenant left then came back with the file on Kenyan. He slapped it on the table, opened it up and showed Terron an old surveillance picture with him and Kenyan.

"You can't lie to me buddy. You know I questioned you about him before."

Terron looked at the picture and said, "Oh I remember dude. He dead?" A guilty smile flashed across Terron's face. The agents on the inside and the outside of the room knew that he was playing games with them.

"I don't know what you're talking about. I need to call my lawyer."

"No need, you're free, for now anyway."

Terron smiled all the way out of the building. He left feeling untouchable, he knew they couldn't do anything to him. He had stopped smiling when he had got back to his car, he was really having a bad day.

He pulled up to the circle and saw Nadia walking by looking good.

"What's up Nadia, where you going?"

"I'm going to my mom's. Where you coming from looking all good," Nadia asked checking Terron out?

"I just came from court," he said grabbing on his suit jacket. "When are we going to get together, you be bullshitting? What, you don't mess with guys at all?"

"No, I don't, but I like you though. Roxy real possessive but she treats me good."

"I'm saying if you happy I'll leave you alone."

"No, I'ma give you a call. I still have ya number."

"Use that thing then."

"I am."

"Promise?"

"I promise."

"Can I get a hug?"

Nadia gave Terron a hug. At first he had his hand on the small of her back, but then he slid them down to her butt. He didn't squeeze, just placed them there.

"Get the fuck off ma girl," Big Roxy said grabbing his shoulder and turning him around with the force of a man. Nadia put her hand over her mouth in shock. She knew she was busted. Terron was shocked not knowing who was grabbing him like that. When he seen it was her, he said, "bitch why the fuck you keep touching me. You know how much this suit cost?"

"I got ya bitch. What I tell you about pushing up on my girl?"

Roxy had her finger pointed directly in Terron's face causing him to slap the shit out of her. SLAP! It was a forceful slap, like a punch. Big Roxy's head whipped to the right, she stumbled back a little, shook it off and put up her hands like a dude. Terron laughed, he couldn't believe that he was about to square up with a chick. She didn't hesitate, she swung some hard shit at him. He backed out of the way and started beating the brakes off of her. She fell to the ground, and he started kicking her in her ribs, chest and back, stumping her out like a dude. He had some hard bottoms on, so she was really hurting.

"You want to act like a fucking dude, I'm going to treat you like one, you stupid bitch."

"Somebody help, get him off of me. Help, make him stop." The true bitch came out of her when she was getting stumped out.

"Please stop Terron, you going to kill her," Nadia pleaded.

"You lucky you not really a dude because I would of bodied you," he said after he stopped.

Nadia helped Big Roxy up and they left. Terron was looking at himself wiping his clothes off. "That bitch made me mess my shoes up," he said to himself.

****

Parked in the cut, Raheem watched the whole thing with his soldiers. "I can't believe he beat that girl like that. Go get him."

Terron was walking back to his car when he looked and seen two dudes with guns in their hands trying to creep up on him.

"Oh shit," he said taking off running. He couldn't go as fast as he wanted in those shoes, but he still was haul assing. They were shooting at him trying to take him out.

Raheem usually didn't get involved in putting in work, he been pass that stage but he wanted Terron for how he did Kenyan. He didn't want to let him get away.

Terron was jumping fences, going through allies and people back yards. He came out on this street and

Raheem pulled up on him. Raheem reached over opening the passenger door. "Get in," he yelled to Terron.

Terron pulsed for a second. His life was on the line. He was desperate, but he felt something wasn't right. He locked eyes with Raheem. Raheem had on a concerned face as if he was really trying to help. It didn't feel right for Terron, so he started running from him too. Raheem got out of the car and started shooting at him. "He went that way," Raheem told his soldiers when they came out of the alleyway. It was too late, Terron had lost them.

Terron spent two hours in his hiding spot before he came out. He left his car but still made it to East Camden to Quick's spot.

"Dam, what the fuck happened to you," Quick asked letting him in?

Terron was looking raggedy. His clothes were dirty, ripped with holes in them. He walked in and plopped on the couch.

"They almost had me," he said wiping his face.

"Who you talking about?"

"Dude Raheem, Kenyan's manz. It's his connect. I didn't think he'll feel any type of way. Shit just got real serious. This dude go in. He got a whole mob of dudes with him, all Muslims.

Terron ran down a little of Raheem's history. The little that he knew about him and his dudes. He never forgot about what happened to Chad. He told Quick that story too.

****

The next day Terron and Quick rode to the circle in two cars, eight dudes, strapped up and ready to go in. When they pulled over, they all got out and posted up just in case anything went down. Like fifteen dudes who was out there came over to Terron while he was getting in his car. They wanted to know what was up.

"What's good Shaytan, I heard about that shit that happened. I'm ready to get saucy. I'm strapped right now, if them dudes come back," Trig said.

"Tonight, we going to get together at the spot, around eight. Be there," Terron aka Shaytan said. Only gang members called him Shaytan. "I need you dudes to stay out here though." Terron was talking to the dudes who was just trappers and weren't affiliated with them. They were mostly dudes who was originally from the circle. They were lucky he still let them trap out there since they chose not to get down with the movement. The few that did get down was welcomed to come.

Shoot First was standing right next to Terron when he told the regular trappers that. He was looking at them like they were enemies. He was always ready to go in. At first dudes was sleeping on him but he was putting in work, showing dudes that he wasn't to be messed with. Mont wasn't aware of the work he had been putting in. He was one of the trappers from the circle who seen him as just a white boy who was out of pocket. When Shoot First was staring at them like they were Enemies, Mont was staring back at him thinking the same thing.

****

Dudes were coming in back to back, but everybody was on time. By 8:30 pm thirty five dudes was packed in the living and dining room of this house. Smoke was everywhere as dudes passed Dutches around. Terron came down the stairs smirking as he seen how many soldiers him and Quick had accumulated. They had grown substantially since he'd been home and they were still growing, in and out of prison.

"I hope y'all ready to put some work in because we got some real problems."

"I'm ready," one dude said.

"It's whatever," another said.

"Let's go," somebody else said.

"Any of y'all know somebody name Raheem? He older, got the big beard with the waves, tall Muslim dude."

A lot of their soldiers were young, early twenties, so they didn't know a lot of the older guys who was getting money behind the scenes. All they knew was the dudes who was on the scene showing people how much money they were getting. Not one of them knew who Terron was talking about except Two Gunz.

"I know who you talking about, he got a truck, right?"

"He probably do, he probably got all kinds of shit but he was in a car the last time I seen him."

"That's him, he always in something different. What's up with him?"

"That's the enemy. Wherever you see him, get him, S.O.S (shoot on site). It don't matter who with him."

Terron knew that he wasn't going to be able to chill with Raheem hunting him down. He chose to go head up with him. During the meeting he told all his dudes to be on point and made plans to do some missions of his own. Two Gunz told them the little he knew about Raheem, and they went off of that. When Terron was done talking he received a phone call.

"Hello."

"Terron, it's me Nadia. Can you come get me?"

"You alright?"

"No, please come get me. I'm at the gas station across the street from the graveyard on Mt. Ephraim."

"Alright, give me fifteen minutes."

The meeting was over. Dudes were just standing around talking.

"I'm out, I gotta make a run. I'll get with y'all."

"No doubt, be safe."

"Alright," Terron said before leaving.

When Terron left the house, it was raining hard. He pulled up to the gas station and seen Nadia standing there in a raincoat with a hood over her head. She had her arms crossed. He could tell that she was freezing. Terron got out of the car and jogged through the rain to her.

"What's wrong?" He seen her face and didn't need an answer. He gently pulled the hoodie off of her head. "Dam, what happened to you?"

Nadia's beautiful face was badly beaten. She had two black eyes, and lumps all over her face. It looked like she got jumped by men. She couldn't even answer his question. She bust out in tears, leaned her head forward and cried on his chest, hugging him. Terron stood there holding her.

****

Quick and his dudes finally decided to disperse. Most of them was outside of the house talking but none of them seen the black GMC truck parked across the street.

Doom Doom, dot dot dot! Dudes hit the ground scrabbling. The three dudes shooting were walking towards the crowd spraying everything. One of the dudes who had got hit had fell into Quick causing him to fall. He seen that dude was out of it, so he grabbed dude and used him as a shield. He looked over and seen Shoot First on his stomach looking around. They caught eye contact and without saying anything both agreed that they had to get out of there.

Shoot First took his gun off of his hip. Quick pushed the dead man off of him and pulled out his gun.

Both got up and took off running firing back without looking. The dudes didn't chase them, they turned their guns their way and began spraying. They let off over a hundred shots in what seemed like twenty five minutes but was really only about two. Afterwards they ran back to the truck and the driver who was still in there sped off.

CHAPTER 27

That night Nadia had told Terron how her head was hurting, so he ended up taking her to the hospital for medical attention. For a minute the nurses thought that he did that to her. She told them he didn't, but they still called the cops. They came in asking a bunch of questions, checking Terron's hands. They came to the conclusion that he didn't beat her. They tried to get her to say who did it, but she wouldn't. Then they got a call on their walkie talkies that had them running out of there.

The doctor diagnosed Nadia with a concussion. Big Roxy had Really did her dirty. She told Terron everything that happened. He felt bad for her, especially because it was over him. That night he took her to his crib and tucked her in. She slept like a baby.

****

"We are here on the corner of Utah street where a massacre of some sort occurred. Five men were shot dead, and eight others were badly wounded. Neighbors reported hearing loud machine guns firing. When the police responded they found multiple men laid scattered on the sidewalk and street. One neighbor reported a wounded man banging on her door asking for help. So far, the police don't have any suspects or leads of what actually took place. I'm Ali Comell with channel 6 news."

The shooting made every newspaper and new channel in the tri state. The hood was on fire. To the police it was clearly gang related because most of the dudes who had gotten shot had red on. They automatically assumed that it was their arch enemies, but they didn't really have a clue about what was going on. They kept leaning on the victims in the hospital hoping they could scare some info out of them, but they held up.

****

Nadia opened her eyes and lifted her head off of Terron's hairy chest. She didn't feel right waking up to him after waking up to a woman for so long. Her movement caused Terron to wake up.

"You alright," he asked?

She looked him over and seen that he only had his boxers on, then she looked at herself and was glad to see that she still had all her clothes on. It was a relief, but she still had to ask.

"Did we…..?"

"What," Terron asked?

"You know, do anything?"

"Nah," Terron said smiling. I wouldn't hit that with ya face looking like that. Plus, if I did you would have remembered."

Nadia tried to laugh but her whole head was hurting. "Ah," she said grabbing her head.

"Lay down, I'll go make you some tea and get you some Advil. That medication they gave you at the hospital had you knocked out."

Nadia watched Terron leave the room. She made herself comfortable in his soft bed. She looked around and seen that everything was set up nice and it was clean. On the dresser was two stacks of money laying there. The average hood chick would have thought about peeling a few dollars from it, but Nadia wasn't a scoundrel. She turned to the side and cuddled up to the pillow.

When Terron came back in the room the first thing he looked at was his money. He had sat it there a certain way. It was the first test. At First glance it looked good, but he still wouldn't know until after he counted it. Back in the day Suki used to be peeling him for all type of money. He knew, he just never said anything because she had him pussy whipped.

"Here you go."

"All you so nice," Nadia said sitting up to receive the tea. She was all smiles.

"I'm saying, it gets better if you ma baby. I really like you but I'm out on bail. I'm going to have to go back in."

"How much time do you have to do?"

"I don't know yet."

"Well, we can deal with that when it gets here, for now I want to be your baby."

"I like the sound of that" Terron sat on the bed, and they talked until he received a phone call.

"Yo," he said answering his phone.

"It's me bro, shit went down last night. You ain't hear?"

"What happened?"

"Come to ma crib, I'll fill you in. Make sure you got that tool with you."

****

"Yo, them dudes tried to murder us all. They killed Trig and like four other homies. It's like eight more dudes in the hospital."

"What," Terron asked shocked?

"Yeah, me and Shoot First barely made it out of there. We went out banging back. I don't know how they knew that we were meeting at that crib, but we gotta find out. Somebody ain't right."

"Yeah, you right," Terron said looking like he was trying to figure things out.

CHAPTER 28

Shoot First walked in the bathroom and turned the faucet on. He splashed some water on his face, then looked at himself in the mirror. He wore the face of a worried man. He couldn't remember being as scared as he was the night they were getting shot at. That was the closest he ever been to death. He was from the suburbs where it didn't go down at all. Even though he had been chilling in the hood and was doing dirt he never was on the other side of the gun until that night. Every dude that had been on the other end of the gun knew that it was two different feelings.

Shoot First began questioning his lifestyle. He began to feel like he was in over his head messing with dudes from Camden. This was their regular. He was raised with a silver spoon in his mouth, he just went astray. He was always considered a bad boy by his friends, family and in school which lead to his incarceration. This was different, he knew it, that's why he decided that he should fall back from Camden for a couple of days.

****

"I got a spot for you if you don't want to go back out there," Raheem said.

"I'm back out there like it's nothing. I don't think they suspect that it was me," Mont said.

"You sure, you could get ya own money. More than you making right now."

"I want that block, plus I want dude just as much as you do. Kenyan was ma bro too. We going to get rid of him and his dudes. He got all these dudes around making shit hot. I don't know none of these dudes. They ain't come up with us, they gotta go."

Mont wasn't feeling Terron or any of the dudes he was bringing around. Most of them was from out East. They weren't the type of dudes he like dealing with and they were all in the circle now. Mont had started trapping in the circle when Terron was locked up. When he came home him and Terron had gotten to know one another but Kenyan was Mont's manz. That's who had put him on. When Kenyan got killed, he had a feeling that Terron had something to do with it. Right after Kenyan's death Terron started flashing, buying new cars like he was celebrating instead of grieving. Then he started bringing a bunch of new gang members out there and was trying to make the people who was from out there get down.

Mont never heard Terron mention what happened to Kenyan. After he had got shot at Mont had heard Terron Talk about how it was Raheem and his dudes. He knew Raheem, so he knew that Raheem had figured out the samething. What really took the cake for Mont was when Shoot First iced grilled him. Mont knew Raheem from Kenyan, he put him on the meeting he heard them talking about. He also put him on where Terron's aunt stayed.

****

Nadia stayed with Terron all week. He took her shopping. She didn't have to worry about any clothes. They were spending time together, getting to know one another. When she healed up, she was back to her beautiful self. He started taking her out to eat and to other places she hasn't experienced. The time he spent with her was him basically trying to get away from the drama he had going on in the city.

Terron and Quick agreed to lay low because they were hot. Their names had kept coming up in the streets and the detectives wanted to question them. Not as suspects, but just because they heard that they were at that house that night. For strategic reasons they decided not to retaliate right away.

Nadia had forgot how good it felt to be with a man. As Terron drilled her from the back she bit the pillow in ecstasy. Each and every stroke reminded her of how good it felt. After Terron bust off, he clasped. She laid on her stomach and he laid there on top of her.

"This pussy good, I'm never letting this thing go."

Nadia started laughing.

"It's nothing like the real thing, huh?"

"Boy you stupid, hush," she said giggling.

They both started laughing. Terron rolled over on his back, she leaned across his chest and had her face close to his.

"When we going to go get my clothes from Roxy's house. It's some other stuff I have to get too."

"Where are you going to take your stuff too?"

"My mom's."

Terron looked at her pretty little face, even though he really wasn't beat he didn't deny her. "I'll take you later."

****

Terron leaned against the car watching Nadia go in and out of the house taking her stuff to the car. Big Roxy followed her every move, telling her that she loved her while begging her to come home. Nadia wasn't beat. Big Roxy shot Terron some hard rocks every time Nadia came out to put something in his car. He stared back stone face. He was unfazed. He couldn't believe that she was still acting tough after that ass whooping he gave her. She must didn't know how easy it was for her to get bodied. He wasn't trying to go that far with her though.

"That's it baby, come on," Nadia told Terron.

Big Roxy almost shed a tear when she heard Nadia call him baby. She stood there looking at them as they both got in the car. Before they could pull off a car pulled up to the passenger side where Nadia was seated and began firing. As soon as Terron seen them he bailed out of the car. The car tried chasing him, but he hit the alley and was gone.

When the shooters pulled off Big Roxy had came from behind the car she was hiding behind. She went back to the car and seen that Nadia had been shot up. She called the cops and tried to help her out as best as possibly.

"Come on baby, keep your eyes open. You're going to make it," Roxy said holding Nadia in her arms. "Don't close ya eyes, look at me. God help us," Big Roxy said looking up. She really cared about Nadia, and it showed. She was crying the whole time while trying to keep Nadia alive. The ambulance finally came and took Nadia to the hospital.

When the police questioned Big Roxy she told them everything. From the description of the car to how Terron had left Nadia. The police towed Terron's car and was now looking for him for questioning.

"It's me, come get me. I'm in this alleyway off of tenth. I don't know the name of the street. I'll see you when you ride down the block."

"What are you doing there," Quick asked?

"Mothafuckas tried to off me. I'll fill you in when you get here."

The pressure was on and Terron was feeling it. He couldn't even show his face without dudes trying to knock his head off. They were on his heels. He couldn't figure out how they kept knowing his where abouts. He knew it was messed up how he left Nadia, but he quickly got over that as he saw Quick's car coming down the street. He came out of the alleyway so Quick could see him. Quick stopped, he got in the passenger, and they kept it moving.

"It's on bro. These dudes ain't letting up, I'm going in, fuck falling back."

"What happened," Quick asked as he turned the corner?

"They pulled up on me. Hit the chick I was messing with up. I don't know if they killed her or not, I wasn't trying to look back."

"Alright, we going all the way in then."

Quick didn't like how they kept coming, making them look like some victims. He was feeling the pressure as well. The city was already talking about what happened to his dudes. That was basically half of his squad. Dudes from other sets weren't getting involved. Everybody was sitting back waiting to see how they would react. So far, they weren't looking good.

CHAPTER 29

"Hello."

"Yo, we need you bro. Come out here," Quick told Shoot First who was enjoying the comfort of the suburbs with this Camden chick he was tender for. They were sitting on the couch in front of the big screen tv watching a movie when he received that call. At the moment he didn't have any worries in the world. He knew no one was bringing that drama to his neck of the woods.

"What's up, everything good?"

"Not at all, so come suited up."

That's all Shoot First needed to hear. He left O girl there alone. Before he showed up to Quick's house, he had shook the jitters and nervousness off. He showed up in all black, with a vest and some gloves on.

"Bout time," Quick said answering the door for him. "I was starting to think you was scared or something."

"Never that, I'm here. Ma name ain't Shoot First for nothing. Let's get right."

Terron, Quick and Shoot First sat out on their journey. It was a reason they didn't want anyone else to tag along.

Click clack. "These dudes are supposed to be God fearing men," Terron said cocking his gun back after he had put the fifty round drum on it. "They trying to get at me, I'ma make them meet God. Turn right here. Yeah, this the corner right here."

Terron remembered going through there a few times with Kenyan. He never got a chance to see what house Kenyan went in, but he knew that he was in the right area. It was around Eleven at night. Only about six hours after Terron had gotten shot at.

"I see somebody on the steps over there, pull up," Terron said Anxiously.

The part of the hood they were in was real quiet. Nobody ever came through there with drama. Terron was about to change that. He knew that they thought things were sweat, like everybody was supposed to respect that it was more of an Islamic community. Not when they were trying to put him down.

They got out and left the car running. Quick crossed the street. It was a cold night. Dude sat on the step bundled up in a bobble coat talking on his cellphone. When he seen Terron and Shoot First he dropped his phone, got up and tried to run in the house, but they tore him up. Every shot echoed loudly throughout the quiet neighborhood. Quick stood on the other side of the street looking out. Dude had about thirty holes in him. He slid down the door and laid there. Terron and Shoot First looked around then quickly started stepping real fast to the car. They wanted someone else to come out, but no one did. They got in the car and sped off. Before they turned the corner someone came out of nowhere and started shooting at them.

"Stop, let me out," Terron said.

"You sure," Quick asked?

"Yeah, stay right here. I'll be right back," Terron said. He opened the car door then took off running. "Go watch his back," Quick told Shoot First.

Terron turned the corner running full speed with his gun in hand. He seen the dude that was shooting at them, but dude didn't see him. He was walking in the direction of the body of the dude they had put down. Terron started shooting at dude. Dude took off running, bussing back without looking. His shots were sounding like firecrackers compared to the ones that was getting sent his way. Terron bent down on one knee and took aim. Dude hit the ground. He started trying to walk dude down, but he heard shots coming from a different direction. He began shooting back at them. Shoot First came along side him and began shooting at them too. They backed out of there and made their way back to their car.

****

Raheem, what's going on? It's a mess out there. The police are everywhere asking questions. One brother is dead, another is in the hospital. What is going on?"

"I'ma take care of it Sheik."

"That's what you were been supposed to do. The last thing we want is heat. It's not good when you're trying to get money. You're supposed to handle that immediately, then get back to business. These guys are nobodies. Do you need some help? Do you want me to make a phone call?"

"That's not necessary. I got everything under control. Trust me."

"Can you do it quietly?"

"I'll try," Raheem said with his head hanging low. He was that dude in the eyes of others, but Anwar was his old head. He didn't want to disappoint him. He knew that things weren't going to get quieter but even louder.

****

Raheem had his dudes staking out the circle and Terron aunt's house. He also had Mont on point for him. Terron wasn't showing his face, but the circle was still selling his product. One day Terron's dudes was taking the work back and forth out East. Raheem's dudes followed them to the crib on 27th street. They ran in there and bodied both of them.

Terron's squad was getting wiped out. It was only about thirty of them. Between them getting shot, killed, locked up, or just falling back. It was only a few of them left. He eventually lost the circle. Raheem had his dudes out there every day. The dudes who were out there who was gang banging started going back out East, and the dudes who wasn't started getting money with Mont. Terron and Quick was feeling trapped. They couldn't show their faces anywhere. They felt like their world was closing in on them, so they took a ride up north to Newark.

****

"Ma CMD homies, what's this problem y'all having down there," Hood asked?

"Some bs, but it's messing up money. That's why we haven't been able to buy what we usually buy," Quick said.

"From what I'm hearing it ain't no bs."

"You're right, that's why we're here. We're at war and we don't have the numbers. Shit not looking good. You know we was building, now dudes don't want to mess with us at all. Not even other sets."

"So, you want me to send some goons down there?"

"Yeah," Quick said. Him, Hood, and Terron continued to talk things over. They needed help, their backs were against the wall. Their numbers were low and they knew eventually that their heads would be on the chopping block.

Eight Newark dudes came back to Camden headed by Flame. All of them had dreads, a look that was foreign to Camden. They were definitely looking out of pocket.

Raheem was rarely seen. Only when he wanted to be. That made it hard for Terron and Quick to get at him. All they knew was that all his dudes were muslims, but that was 70% of the whole Camden. They decided to go to the only place they knew he would be.

It was 1:30 pm, right after Jumu'ah prayer. All the Muslims were leaving the Masjid. It was crowded out front, everyone was socializing, getting in their cars and saying their salaams. Raheem was coming out of the Masjid talking to Wali. Wali was another one of Raheem's dudes. Even though he was from Camden he got money in Burlington. Him and his dudes had something called M.O.E (Muslims Over Everything) going on out there. They had the whole Burlington on smash.

They were having a business conversation when shots rang out. Everybody started scattering, hitting the ground, including Raheem and Wali. Raheem looked up and seen two cars with dudes hanging out of the windows shooting. They had flags over their faces and guns. They peeled off and Raheem got up to see if everyone was ok. Three people were hit. The ambulance came and rushed them to the hospital. Anwar came out of the Majid furious. He knew what it was about. He looked at Raheem with the evil eyes.

Almost every dude who was leaving that Mosque, who they fired upon, either used to be in the mix or was still in the mix. Not to mention people families who was out there. One of the reasons nobody was messing with Terron and Quick in the first place was because they either dealt with Raheem in one way or the other. Respected or feared him or was Muslims themselves, even though they might have had other affiliations. Now they really had beef coming from all angles. People who knew something was coming up to Raheem volunteering and telling him what they were going to do when they caught one of them dudes slipping. This made it hard for them other sets who didn't have anything to do with it.

Just because they were branded the same it was hard for them to eat.

"Y'all did what?"

Terron shook his head when he found out what happened. He wouldn't have gone that far, not at a Masjid. On top of that he considered drive byes to be weak. The wrong person always got hit and the job never got finished. He wanted to send them dudes right back up north.

"We sprayed that shit up. You said you wanted dude Raheem, right?" That was the only spot we could catch him at. I know we got him, I seen him get hit. I told you whenever you need me to put that work in, I got you," Flame said sounding like he just did something super gangsta. He didn't know how upset Terron was because he didn't show it. He looked over at Quick. They both knew that this had went too far. If it wasn't before then it definitely was now.

CHAPTER 30

Anwar received a phone call from one of his close friends in the police department. They met up to have a conversation about what was going on.

"I'm sorry to hear about what happened at the Mosque the other day. I don't know what's going on but it's getting ugly. It's not good for the city. The feds stepped in and started investigating some of the guys that attend your Masjid. They noticed their affiliations with some other guys. I don't know if their investigating you, I don't know who their investigating, but I know you used to be on their radar so be careful. If I could help you out in anyway let me know. It is what you pay me for, right?"

"Let me talk to some people and I'll get back to you," Anwar said.

"Alright, I'm going to do what I can to find out more, but you have to understand that the feds don't share information with us. It's a lot of distrust and tension that go on between us. They do their own thing but I'm on top of everything."

Captain Price had been on Anwar's pay roll for years. He had a whole squad of crooked cops behind him. They all listened to him. Among some of the things they were into was robbing drug dealers, and extortion. Captain Price had come up through the ranks to his current position. He had higher aspirations, he wanted to become commissioner next. Anwar just made sure that Captain Price's squad didn't mess with any of his peoples and that he kept him informed about police activities on street matters.

Anwar left that meeting knowing that things was getting out of control. He relied on Raheem to control the streets. It wasn't supposed to be this much noise over one man's death. If he would have known things would get this serious, he would have told Raheem to let it ride. He called Raheem to his office.

The Escalade Anwar was sitting in was converted into an office on the inside. It had luxury chairs that reclined, a big screen tv, a place for him to put his laptop, a mini refrigerator, and a mini bar amongst other things.

Anwar stared at Raheem as he got in with him. Raheem knew that look, even though he never got it from Anwar before. He knew that it was the look of disappointment. He could feel the truck moving as the driver drove off.

"I'm not going to blame you for what happened, but stuff like that is never supposed to happen."

"I got an S.O.S out on them. Everybody wants their heads for what they did."

Listening to Raheem talk didn't make Anwar feel any better. He was to the point where he was about to suit up and go in himself to show them how it's really done. He was far removed from that though. His game now was all mental. He had plans for his back up plans.

"My sources said that the feds are investigating, so lay low. Get away from the city, because it's on fire. Certain things I can't protect y'all from. It's to that point."

Raheem nodded in agreement, but it was no way he was going to let them dudes live. Not after what they did.

****

The cops had pulled the Newark dudes over out Polock. They seen four dudes in a car with dreads, that was all the reason they needed. It was always a bunch of people roaming the streets out Polock. When something happened people were always trying to be nosey, so they gathered around. The cops had the dudes handcuffed sitting on the curb while they searched the car. Besides looking like they weren't from Camden they all had red on in a Crip area.

It took the dudes a minute to realize it, but as the people gathered around, they seen more dudes in blue than anything else. They come from a gangland, so their eyes were trained to peep stuff like that. This made them nervous. They started communicating amongst themselves, putting each other on point.

Since none of them had license, and the car wasn't insured it was getting impounded. The cop waited until the tow truck took their car, then he gave the driver his tickets with a smile on his face because he knew that he was about to do something grimy. He unhandcuffed them, walked to his car, turned to one of the dudes who wore blue in the crowd and said, "They're all yours."

He pulled off. The dudes started walking in the opposite direction of the crowd. Flame pulled out his phone and called Quick.

"Yo, the cops took our car. We out polock and dudes are on some uhmmm...."

Quick heard a big thump, a lot of wreckers and commotion going on. "Come on, lets go get these dudes," he said putting his gun on his hip. Shoot First and his other two dudes followed him.

They were riding up Louis when they seen the cops, ambulance and a crowd of people looking at whatever had happened. As they got closer, they saw two bodies covered with white sheets. One ambulance had put on their sirens and sped off. Quick decided to follow it to the hospital.

"Hello," Quick said answering his phone.

"Yo, it's me Flame, come get me. I'm in this alleyway on some street called Browning," he said in a low tone.

"Alright, I'm on ma way. You alright?"

"Nah, I'm fucked up."

"Alright, stay on the phone until I get there."

When Quick arrived Flame came out of the alleyway limping with a bloody face. He got in the car leaned back and closed his eyes. He was in obvious pain

"What happened bro?"

Flame didn't answer right away. They went to Quick's house, and he told them how the cops left them for dead in Crip territory.

"You sure you don't want to go to the hospital?"

"Nah, I can't. I'm on the run. I just need some down time."

When the other dudes who Flame came to Camden with found out what had happened, they strapped up and went to work. They went out Polock and murdered somebody then went back to Newark.

****

It was a real live war going on. The police were getting more and more info from the streets. Early Tuesday the police simultaneously raided two of Raheem's spots, locking six people up. They got caught with coke and guns. The police tried pressuring them about the killings that were happening, but they held up.

Anwar's connections could no longer protect them. It was too much shooting going on. That wasn't just what them two fractions had going on. It was other things happening in the city which had the city extra hot.

In Anwar's days he would have deaded this situation before it ever got to this point. He had ran through plenty of beefs, so he couldn't figure out how dudes was causing him so much trouble. Drama wasn't good when money was involved. Anwar was a family man with political ties. He couldn't move how he used to. He couldn't let anything lead back to him. Raheem wasn't getting it done how he was supposed to, which caused the Sheik to call in an old friend.

"Hello," Brother Bashir answered.

"As salammu alay kum, It's Anwar."

"Wa alaykum salam. It's good to hear from you Akhie. How you been?"

They haven't spoken in a little over a year. Brother Bashir and Anwar used to run together years ago when Anwar was really getting his hands dirty. Brother Bashir was a part of Anwar's rise to the top. He specialized in giving dudes the death penalty. He been stop selling drugs. He told Anwar that he was getting too old for the nonsense. He never stopped putting in work though. He only did it when called upon. Anwar would reward him handsomely every time.

When Anwar and Brother Bashir got together Anwar filled him in on everything he knew. He only knew what Raheem told him about Terron, Quick, and some white boy. Like where they were from and what they dealt with. Raheem knew what they looked like, he didn't. Bother Bashir had his own way of finding things out. Everything he heard about these guys sounded like child's play.

Bashir was about 5'7, dark skin with a low skintight cut and a big beard that he kept tidy. Nowadays he was a businessman, so he looked the part, but when it was time to put in work, he dressed the part for that too. He hit the ground in a pair of jeans and a black t-shirt that was too big for him but perfect for the roll he was trying to play. He walked down Thorndyke towards Rand Street. At every corner somebody was running up to him trying to sell him drugs.

"I'm good youngen," he told each hustler. When he walked up to Rand Street, he asked them did they have anything.

"Yeah, what's up," one of the dudes asked?

"Let me get two."

Dude gave him two and he gave the dude twenty dollars. He seen this aunti walking down the street with a fat ass.

"What's up baby, you trying to do something," he asked opening his hand showing her the bags he had bought.

"Sure am, where are we going?"

"I'm following you."

"Come on," she said leading the way.

Her ass wasn't really the reason he approached her. She looked like a local fiend, he could tell because the drug dealers wasn't asking her did she want anything. They knew if she wanted something that she'll let them know. Plus, she was trying to game the other fiends. He figured that he would let her think that she had a sucka. She took him in this house, and he gave her a bag.

"Do you be copping off of Rand?"

"No, that's where you got this from?"

"Yeah."

"You should of went to Morse Street. That's where I usually go. They got better stuff."

"Now I know. Who runs that set on Rand?"

"Quick."

"Do he be out there like that?"

"I be seeing him sometimes," she said as she put the pipe to her lips and pulled. "Why," she asked in a changed voice?

After she took a blast, her eyes got real big and red.

"I just might want to buy more."

Once he said that she knew he had money. Which meant she thought she had a sucka. Her plans had changed. At first she was going to smoke all his stuff and not give him any sex, now she figured she could get him for a lot more. She was willing to do whatever to achieve that.

"You trying to buy weight?"

"Something like that, but I was told dudes from Rand had it for cheap. That's why I want to see what's up with them. That's why I bought this stuff first, to see how good it was."

"All baby, I can show you them as soon as we finish," she said hitting the pipe again. She went over towards him and got close. She was so greedy that she didn't realize that he wasn't smoking. He sat there and watched her smoke both bags. He had got a little contact from being so close to her asking all of them questions.

She only knew basic stuff that went on around there. When her high wore off he took her back around there to buy more drugs. This time they sat on some abandoned steps, in clear view of everything happening on Rand Street. She got high as Brother Bashir kept his eyes on the dudes on the block.

"Is that them?"

"Who, where" she asked nervously?

"I'm talking about dude Quick."

"Yup, that looks like him. Him and Terron. I don't know who that white guy is, but he's always with them."

Anwar had expressed how bad he wanted this to end. Brother Bashir definitely knew how to bring things to an end, especially lives.

"Where you going baby," the fiend asked as Brother Bashir got up and started walking.

"I'm going to go get you some more of that good stuff. Don't worry, I'll be back."

Brother Bashir walked up on the group of dudes. He wanted a good visual of his soon to be victims. "Let me get two," he said to the young boy that was standing right next to Quick. He looked Quick straight in the eyes. For a split second it seemed like Quick looked at him too, but it was just a glance, more like he looked through him. To Quick he was just another fiend, he didn't really count.

"Yo mothafucka, you got ya shit now get the fuck out of here. You making shit hot," Shoot First said all in Brother Bashir's face. Bashir looked at him, smirked, and walked away looking at his bags.

"Old dirty mothafucka man," Shoot First kept saying loud enough for him to hear. He didn't know who he was talking to. Brother Bashir took note of his disrespect, he had plans on making him pay for it. He went and gave the fiend chick them two bags then walked to his car and pulled it right down the street from where Quick's car was. He followed all three of them for days.

CHAPTER 31

Terron went to his aunt's house, when he pulled up there was police and ambulance out front. The entrance of the house was taped off. The paramedics came out of the house with a body bag. Terron pulled over and got out of the car and started running towards the house. One of the policemen stopped him.

"This ma aunt's house, I live here," Terron said trying to push past the cop. The cop wasn't having it, he started holding Terron back.

"What's going on here?"

"Lieutenant, this guy is saying he lives there."

Lieutenant Lynch looked at Terron and smirked. "Let him go," he told the officer. He was happy to see Terron because his name had came up in so much that he wanted to question him.

"This is your aunt's house?"

"Yeah, what happened?"

"I'm sorry to inform you but her and her husband was found dead, shot to death."

"What, nah fuck that," Terron said running over to the ambulance that had the person in the black bag on the gurney.

"Unzip that, let me see who that is."

The paramedic dude looked around nervously. He caught eye contact with Lieutenant Lynch and Lieutenant nodded his head for him to unzip the body bag. The paramedic unzipped the bag and Terron seen his aunt laying there lifeless. He was crushed, he knew that it was because of him that she was dead. He broke down and went over to the step.

Terron felt like he killed his aunt himself. He couldn't believe that things had went this far. He thought that by moving out of the hood he was good. That he could do his dirt and dudes couldn't touch him, but he never planned on going up against the dudes he was up against. He didn't think to get his peoples out of the hood too. He just sat there looking down at the ground. Lieutenant Lynch watched him. He was enjoying Terron's misery. He seen many cases like this before, he ain't have no sympathy for someone who was supposed to be a cold blooded murderer. What he did know was that Terron was looking real vulnerable. He went over to him and put his hand on Terron's shoulder. "I'ma need you to come to the station. I got a lot of questions for you."

He said it as if Terron didn't have a choice. Terron got up and he walked Terron to his unmarked car and put him in the back seat unhand cuffed. Terron laid down and put his arm over his face. He was really stressing over what happened to his aunt.

At the station they were asking questions but couldn't get anything out of him. He wasn't talking at all. He was tired and zoned out. He felt like the life had been sucked out of him. He sat there with red watery eyes looking through the Lieutenant as he asked questions and then pounded on the table because Terron wouldn't answer him. Lieutenant Lynch threated him in every way, including getting his bail revoked, but it all fell on deaf ears. Terron seen the Lieutenant moving around angrily and heard his voice, but nothing he was saying.

"What are we going to do? He's not saying anything," one of the fat agents said.

"I hate these kinds of guys. They stick to these fake codes that don't mean anything," Agent John said.

"Get the warrant so we could tap his phone, tail him everywhere, he's going to slip up. We just have to make sure we stay on him."

They let Terron leave the station six hours later. He walked from downtown police station back to Whiteboy Fairview. He walked through the circle and seen the dudes that was out there hustling, but he didn't say anything to them. He hadn't had coke out there in months. Mont had the block now and he was getting coke from Raheem. When Mont seen Terron coming through he thought that he was on some other stuff. Mont knew about what happened to his aunt. It took place a few blocks from where they be, so everybody knew. He watched as Terron Turned the corner then he called Raheem.

When Terron turned the corner there was a medical van parked in front of Roxy's house. He didn't really pay It any mind. He happened to look up and see Big Roxy and the driver unloading Nadia from the van onto the sidewalk. Him and Nadia made eye contact. Her eyes followed him, but she couldn't move her head. She was now a paraplegic, paralyzed from the neck down. Big Roxy looked to see who she was looking at. She looked at Terron and Rolled her eyes. Terron didn't pay her any mind, but he did feel bad for Nadia.

When Terron got to his aunt's house it was one cop still parked out front doing paperwork. Terron sat in his car which was down the street. It took about fifteen minutes for the cop to leave. Terron sat there looking at the house still sad. He grabbed his gun from under the seat and put it on his lap. He was ready to get out of the car when two dudes ran up on the driver side door and started shooting the car up. Before Terron knew what was going on the bullets were tearing through his flesh. He started shooting back, dropping one dude. He jumped in the passenger seat and made it out the door. The other dude kept firing. Terron hid behind the car, he didn't really know where dude was exactly. He was starting to feel the pain from the shots that hit him, especially from the ones that hit his gut. He took off running.

The dude who he had put down started shooting at him. He shot Terron in the leg causing him to fall. The other dude seen that as an opportunity and tried to come from behind the car on him, but Terron seen him and started shooting. In the middle of the gun battle the police came from every direction.

Terron was never happier to see them. He breathed a sigh of relief. He slid his gun under the closest car and stretched his hands out and started yelling, "help, I need medical attention."

He knew that he was hit up bad, he felt at least five points of burning sensations on his body. The police locked all three of them up. They found all of the guns that were involved. They took Terron and the guy that was wounded to the hospital and kept a heavy police presence there to make sure nothing happened. The guy who wasn't wounded went straight to the county.

****

The newspapers and the news channels blew the whole thing up. The two dudes were not only charged wIth attempted murder on Terron, but now they were suspects in the murder of his aunt and her husband.

Quick and Shoot First was upset about what happened to Terron. They were hoping that he pulled through. They were losing and they knew it. They couldn't even get money. They had to creep through the hood because they were afraid that if someone seen them that they would alert the enemies and dudes would be on their way. For the most part they played the out skirts where Shoot First lived. Out there it was drama free.

"Yo, we might as well play out here until things cool down in Camden. It's not like we're missing anything. We're not making money out there. The police are all over us and every time we're out there we always have to watch our backs. At least out here we know we're good. We could get money with ease, party and run through these broads," Shoot First said.

"You're right. I'ma fall back for a while, but I can't let them dudes think that they won. I ain't going out like that. I got a rep I gotta uphold," Quick responded.

He was right, Shoot First really didn't understand. He didn't care what went on in Camden, nobody knew him out there. He could forget everything that they went through and keep moving about his life. Quick couldn't, he knew the hood was talking negatively about how him and his dudes were getting ran out of the city. His pride was in the way. Dudes like him couldn't stand not being spoken highly of. The fact that dudes was speaking badly about him was eating him up. He was willing to put it all on the line before he went out like that.

"We're going to stay out here, get this money right, recruit more dudes, then I'ma ease back into the hood and make it happen. I'ma knock dudes off on the low this time."

That plan might of made sense to Quick, but Shoot First was getting tired. Quick grew up in drama, he didn't. He was seeing dudes around him get killed and he wasn't trying to be one of them, nor was he trying to go back to prison. He kept his thoughts and feeling to himself though.

****

Raheem bailed his dudes out and told them to fall back. He knew that they were being investigated because the police was trying to get them for murdering Terron's aunt. That made them extra hot. Raheem didn't want them anywhere around. At the same time, he made sure they were good.

Things got quiet when Quick and Shoot First decided to stay out of the city. At least their beef did anyway. It was other things going on in the hood, but Rand Street was shut down and Mont had the circle. He was getting his work from Raheem.

Everything was back to normal for Raheem, he was moving back how he was supposed too. Anwar wasn't on him because his peoples were calm. There wasn't anything messing with their money.

Terron stayed in the hospital for about a month. When he got better, he was taken to the county jail. He had to be on the medical block because he had a shit bag and was in a wheelchair. They revoked his bail, and he was charged with attempted murder for shooting dude. New Jersey didn't have a self defense law, especially not for the black man. For them it was better to kill two birds with one stone. Terron's whole world was upside down. He knew he wasn't coming home anytime soon. He never felt pain how he was feeling at the present moment. It was in his heart. He had gotten himself in a jam that he couldn't get of.

The nurse came on the cell block for med call. Dudes were beasting, lining up, looking like they were copping dope. It was mostly fiends trying to get their hands on something close to what they used to use on the streets. Hurt up or not Terron still had his pride. Plus, he knew the nurse who was serving the meds. They went to school together. He hated for her to see him like this.

"Hey Terron," she said when she finally got to him.

"What's up Indie?"

He wouldn't even have spoken to her if she wouldn't of said something to him first.

"Terron, if you need anything let me know. I got you."

"Alight, I appreciate that."

Indie felt bad seeing him in the condition he was in. She gave him his pills and a cup. He drank it and she didn't even try to see if he really swallowed them or not like she was required to do from all the inmates. The c.o. didn't say anything either, they just left. Terron watched her ass jiggle away in them scrubs thinking about how he could have been hit, but now he might not ever get a chance to.

He rolled his wheelchair over to the phones and called Shoot First.

"Hello."

Terron could tell that it was a white chick that answered the phone by her voice, but he knew the one Shoot First usually kept around, and it didn't sound like her.

"Put Shoot First on the phone."

"Who's That? You mean Timothy?"

"Bitch, give me the phone," Shoot First said grabbing the phone from her. "Get ya fat ass out of here," he said and smacked her cheeks making them sound off.

"Ouch," she said rubbing her butt. She had panties on, thats it.

"Yo bro, what's up?"

"Nothing, what y'all doing?"

"Getting fucked up. It's like girls gone wild over here. Bunnies everywhere, drunk as hell, licking each other. Today my birthday so we're having a little party. What's up though, you need anything?"

"You can't get me what I really need. Shit ain't looking too good for me. Where Quick at?"

"Right here, hold on." Shoot First gave Quick the phone. He was feeling for Terron, he knew that he was talking about freedom. He knew that he'll be alright though.

"What's good bro, how you feeling," Quick asked?

"Not too good."

"You good man, you still living. That's all that matters."

"Yeah, but these mothafuckas coming for ma head. You know I'ma handle mines. I'm just trying to get the right deal because I'm not taking these things to trial. Especially not that old body again. Anything is better than what I had before."

"You right, you know we going to do real shit on our end. You ain't going to have to worry about anything. That's my word. Don't nothing change, you still hold up in there, I got out here."

Terron and Quick talked about the whole situation like it was nothing, but the other side of the game to them. When their fifteen minutes was up Quick went back to partying.

Months later Terron was on a regular tier. His condition was much better. Besides the occasional aches and pains, he was good. The c.o. was escorting him to meet with his lawyer. He walked in the little office and sat down.

"How are you doing Mr. Walls?"

"Could be better."

"Well, I'm here to advise you of the plea bargain the prosecutor offered. Would you be willing to plea out to a 20 with 85%?"

Terron scrunched up his face.

"Now before you give me your answer, as your lawyer I must advise you 20 with 85% for all of these charges isn't that bad if you think about it. You had 45 years to life. Then you got locked up for an attempted murder on top of these other charges. That makes everything really look bad, and for whatever reason this prosecutor acts like he really has it out for you. I advise you to take it, but the decision is yours to make."

When Terron's lawyer told him about the prosecutor having it out for him he thought maybe it had something to do with how much the feds wanted him. Even though he hesitated he didn't have to think long, he knew things wasn't in his favor.

"I'll take it," he said.

"Alright, I'll let the prosecutor know and get back in touch with you. I should have you in court in a few days."

Terron went back to the tier, called his peoples to tell them how much time he just copped out to.

"Hello," Quick answered.

"What's good bro?"

"What's good, Hood was asking about you. We just came back from taking that trip up north. I took Shoot First up there and them dudes thought he was the feds until Hood vouched for him."

Quick was laughing while Shoot First sat in the passenger seat salty about the whole thing.

"I took twenty bro."

"You took twenty? That ain't bad compared to what they was trying to give you. They're giving you time served for that time you did before you got back on the appeal, right?"

"Yeah."

"Oh, you good, I thought they were going to hang you. I ain't going to lie. Remember this ya second time getting caught red handed. I remember when we was down you told me that they caught you with the burner before."

"You're right."

"I'm saying, how much you did before?"

Almost seven. I'ma have over ten to do because you do like seventeen and some change off of 20 with 85%.

"That's nothing, we going to have you sitting right when you come home. The hood was hot. We had came out here to the outskirts for a minute, but we back out there now."

After months in hiding Quick was back in the hood. He opened Rand Street back up and was trying to get his numbers up to make an army. He still was laying low and playing the outskirts heavy because Terron warned him about how them boys was mentioning his name while trying to squeeze info out of him. Plus, he wasn't dumb enough to think that the beef was over because some time had went by. Not the kind of beef they had going on. He had got rid of all the cars he was known for driving and was now driving all tinted up rentals.

CHAPTER 32

Halloween night in the city was packed with kids trick or treating. Some had their parents with them, most didn't. It was a few groups walking around with cops. They had the little lime green glow sticks. The cops that were with them were their guides and protectors, but their presence didn't move any of the drug dealers from posting up on the blocks. It was just for some reason during mystery night and Halloween the crime always seem to skyrocket. It was more police on the streets to look out for the kids.

"Yo, hand me that plate."

Shoot First handed Quick the plate. Quick took the coke out of the pot and put it on the plate. Then took the baking soda that was already in the baggy weighed up and started pouring it on the coke, then started whipping it up, mixing it in.

"We should keep one of these all powder. We almost ran out last time," Shoot First said. "Plus, I got a few people who want powder, they buying ounces. I'm charging them top dollar for it too."

He convinced Quick. "Alright, we can double up on that."

One good thing about that outskirts flow was that Camden nicks were dimes out there, and in some cases twenties depending on how fat the nicks were. They also charged more when they sold weight.

"Who is that ringing the bell," Quick asked as he continued to whip up the coke.

"I got it."

While Shoot First went to see who it was, Quick couldn't help but to think that shouldn't nobody be ringing the doorbell because shouldn't nobody know that they were there.

"It's just a kid trying to trick or treat," Shoot First said after peeking out the window.

"Tell his little ass to get the fuck out of here. We ain't got no treats for him, unless he smoke yay."

"I should break him off something and put it in his bag," Shoot First said laughing. When he finally opened the door and looked down at the trick or treater in the Spiderman costume, he was staring down the barrel of a black 45.

The first shot hit him in the face. The ones that followed hit him in the chest, arm, then the side causing him to fall. Brother Bashir stepped over him and entered the house looking for Quick. When Quick heard the shots, he dropped everything and grabbed his gun. As the Spiderman costume assailant tried to enter the kitchen Quick started shooting. Brother Bashir began shooting back with marksmen aim. He hit Quick in the abdomen twice. Quick felt it but kept shooting until

Brother Bashir ran out of the door. That's when Quick grabbed his stomach. He took a knee because the pain was ripping him.

The front door was still open when the police showed up. They had their weapons drawn, not knowing what to expect. The first person they seen was Shoot First laying on the floor. When they seen that he was still alive they dispatched an ambulance. A few more police made their way in the house, that's when they seen Quick.

"Freeze, get your hands up," one cop said.

"I can't," Quick said real low.

They bum rushed him, jumping on him, even though he was already on the ground.

"AAhhh," was all he could yell as they bent him up and put him in hand cuffs. They sent both of them to the hospital. They had three bricks of coke out in the open. Once the cops seen that, they searched the house finding weed and guns.

Even though Shoot First injuries were severe the doctors were still able to save him. Quick wasn't so lucky. The bullet had hit a main artery and he died.

Shoot First had got shot in the face, but some how it didn't hit his brain. It came out of his neck. He also had a bullet still lodged in the left side of his back. Everyday a cop stood outside of his hospital room, but he wasn't aware of it yet. He was in critical condition. It took him three months to come around. When he did a cop was right there to read him his rights. He got charged with everything in the house. When the feds found out that he was going to survive they stepped in and paid him a visit.

"Timothy Burnet, I'm Lieutenant Lynch and this is agent John."

Shoot First Made a grimacing face as he struggled to sit up.

"I have to ask you, what are you, a white boy doing in this dangerous city? You're in the hood at that, with a house full of drugs," Lieutenant Lynch asked looking at him for a few seconds for a response? Shoot First looked at him like he wasn't interested in entertaining his question. Lieutenant Lynch smirked, he knew he was a want to be tough guy.

"I guess you don't want to talk about it. I'm going to help you out. I know all that stuff in that house wasn't yours so whose was it?"

"All what stuff? I don't know what you are talking about."

"You can act like you got amnesia, but you only playing with your own life. You think I'm here for nothing."

Shoot First really didn't remember much from that night. Lieutenant Lynch could tell, but he planned on pressing him until his memory came back.

"Do three kilos of cocaine refresh your memory? Two of switch were cooked up. Those are just the major charges. Not to mention we got a gun off of your hip, along with other guns and drugs that was in the house, and guess what? It's all on you. Hope you can handle it, but let me let you in on something. These guys that you hang out with are not your friends. They don't care about you. You see they already tried to kill you, maybe next time you won't be so lucky. Then again there won't be a next time."

He took a couple steps away from the bed and continued, "I met your mother the other day. Nice old lady, you come from a good family, but I had to tell them that you're never coming home."

Shoot First watched them as they left. His mind went blank. Then he began wondering what was up with Quick. He haven't heard anything about him since that night. He didn't know if he got away or what. He figured that since no one was saying anything about him then maybe he did. He grabbed the paper lieutenant Lynch left on his bed and started reading it. Once he got finished, he knew he was fucked. It was a copy of his police report. A couple months later Shoot First was well enough to be taken to jail. He was taken to the federal building over Philly. That's when his court proceedings started. That's when he found out how real things were.

Shoot First Stood there, clean cut, shaved, blonde hair, blue eyes. Some type of gel or moose in his hair that allowed his hair to stay in a style he would have never wore if he wasn't in court. A nervous lump was in his throat as he listened to the judge read the charges. Everything felt surreal. He looked over at the prosecutor as she argued to give him the most time possible. He heard the time he was facing and nothing else. Next thing he knew the sheriff was taking him out of the courtroom.

****

"I hope you got something good to tell me Mr. Burnett. I don't like playing games. Now talk to me," the Lieutenant said as he walked in the room. Shoot First had decided to take the easy wat out.

"None of that stuff was mine. It was all Quicks."

"Who's Quick?"

"His name is David Chamber."

"You're going to mess up your only chance by trying to shift the blame to a dead man."

"Dead," Shoot First questioned? "How did he die?"

"You must don't remember. He got shot by the same person who shot you. He died at the hospital. You still don't know who shot you?"

"No," he said shaking his head. He still was trying to digest the fact that Quick got killed. He realized that he was all alone. Not a person to share that blame with or put the blame on.

"Alright look, I'll tell you where we get the coke from, and about the murders. I'll tell you whatever, as long as I get out of here. I can't do this shit," he said breaking down crying like a baby.

Lieutenant Lynch smiled. Shoot First told everything, from when he first got down with Quick, to the night he had got shot. He told them about their beefs. That he was one of the dudes who shot Kenyan up, how Terron set it up. Then how Terron set the dudes up who went to the hospital and killed Kenyan. All the questions Lieutenant Lynch had was being answered. Shoot First was in deeper than the Lieutenant first expected him to be. He knew everything he said was true because it all made sense.

Lieutenant Lynch took a special interest when he started talking about Terron. When Shoot First was done he had got their whole set indicted. Dudes from Camden, up north, to the dudes that joined them that were from the suburbs where Shoot First was from. The feds rounded all of them dudes up. When they ran down on them, they got caught with other stuff which added to the charges.

Shoot First tried to get the Muslims locked up, but he didn't know enough about them. All he knew was Muslims, he really didn't know exactly who he was beefing with.

****

Terron got his charges hand delivered to him by a c.o..

"What the fuck is this," he asked looking at the papers. He seen three counts of murder charges, drug conspiracy, and all these other charges. As soon as they let him out for rec he called his lawyer. With the charges he was facing it was no way he would see the streets again, not even if he took a plea bargain.

Two years later

From Camden New Jersey to Newark New Jersey, twenty seven dudes had been indicted. Almost all of them had pleaded out. None of their charges were as severe as Terron's. He had to go all the way and hope that he could get back on an appeal.

The trial made headlines because it was gang related. The news was comparing it to a time they took down a local gang called The Sons of Sin that terrorized Camden in the early 90's.

Terron walked in the courtroom in a tailor made suit without any handcuffs. He looked at the chick that was doing his bid with him and gave her a little head nod. Terron took a seat. His lawyer said something to him that nobody else could hear. The judge came out and the court proceeding begun. The judge begun talking, then the prosecutor, then Terron's lawyer gave their opening statements. The prosecutor called the only witness. Shoot First walked in through the door that free people who go to court walk through.

How the hell this dude coming in from the streets, Terron thought to himself.

He sat on the stand. The bailiff put the bible in front of him and told him to put his left hand on it and his right hand up. Shoot First complied. "Do you swear to tell the truth, nothing but the truth, so help you god."

"I do."

Shoot First told them everything. How they met, put the team together and that Terron was the second in charge. He reiterated everything he confessed to Lieutenant Lynch. How they shot Kenyan, killed the dudes over Philly, amongst other bodies. He told how they sold drugs in Camden and up the highway, and where they got it from. He told the jury an elaborate story of sex, money, murder and mayhem in sequence from beginning to end. He had the jury captivated the whole time. It was like he was reading them an amazing novel.

The trial lasted a few days. It only took the jury four hours to come back with a verdict.

"Did the jury reach a verdict," the judge asked?

"Yes your honor," the Forman said standing up. "We the jury fine the defendant guilty on count 1, murder in the first degree. The Forman kept reading off the paper, finding Terron guilty on every charge and count. Terron who was standing up when they first started reading the verdict sat back down in the chair. Two Sheriffs posted up right behind him.

"Okay, I'll schedule sentencing for Friday February 3," the judge said.

The sheriffs told Terron to stand up and put his hands behind his back. He got up and acted like he was going to cooperate, but then tried to grab the sheriffs gun off of his hip. They started tussling, he was pushing the one sheriff back while going for his gun, but the other sheriff was punching on him from the back. He didn't feel any of that. He was too determined to get that gun. He had his hand on it but couldn't get it out of the holster. A few women were screaming, everybody in the courtroom was standing up. The judge had ran back to his chambers. Like six other sheriffs ran in and rushed Terron, taking him to the ground. They started beating him up because he wouldn't stop wilding.

The whole time Brother Bashir sat in the back of the courtroom quietly. No one knew who he was. He witnessed every day of the trial. He knew Terron was going to get found guilty. When they finally got Terron to the ground Brother Bashir slipped outside of the room.

CHAPTER 33

"Now what, I did everything that was asked of me am I free," Shoot First asked?

"You were given immunity for your complete cooperation, so yes you're free."

They were at the safe house that Shoot First was being held at in Harrisburg PA. A couple of agents was there with Lieutenant Lynch to unplug their stuff and disconnect Shoot First from the ankle bracelet monitor they had him on. The case was high profile, so they took cautious measures to make sure that he made it to trial.

For the first time in two years Shoot First was reunited with his family in Jersey. A few days later he received a call from a lady name Jamie Hung asking him would he like to sell the rights to his life story.

"My life story," he asked thinking about it. He was just feeling like he was getting his life back. He was trying to leave everything behind him, but she was offering money and he definitely needed money.

"I'm an author, I been following your case since you got locked up. It intrigued me when I first read it in the newspaper. The only white guy in a black gang. That'll be a big seller. We may can even get you a movie deal.

He really started thinking money when she mentioned a movie deal. How excited he was he probably would have sold his ass for a movie deal. He said yes to everything.

Within six months his book was on the New York's best seller list and Hollywood gave him a movie deal. In his book he went into depth on everything. It started from when he was born, how he grew up, when he met Quick and Terron, their plans, their beefs, and all about his case. The white folks were buying his book up. That's how It made it to the best sellers list. White folks were amazed by the life he was living. To them him surviving the hood was like Tarzan surviving the jungle.

It took another year for the movie to come out. When it did, he attended the premiere. He was on the red carpet taking pictures for the paparazzi, posing like an A list star. Taking pictures with other stars, living it up. After the premiere he went to an after party. Hollywood was holding him up like he was some type of hero, while the dudes he snitched on was in prison doing hard time. Terron had got five life sentences on top of the time he already had.

Shoot First's story made him a few million. He was good. Since he been in Jersey, he settled down with some chick he grew up with. They had a baby on the way. He bought a nice big house, and they moved in together. He opened a business. He was trying to get his affairs in order. He never looked back or thought about his past. His past became like a dream.

It was approximately twelve O' clock at night when Shoot First stepped onto the balcony to smoke a cigarette. Looking at the beautiful scenery, he blew out a long chain of smoke while tilting his head up so the smoke could go up. That's when Brother Bashir put him in the choke hold. He had the UFC fighter choke around his neck. He broke Shoot First down to the ground. He was kicking and trying to peel Brother Bashir's arms off as he lost breath. Brother Bashir put him to sleep then snapped his neck. After doing so he looked up because he heard something.

Shoot First's girl came to the balcony and seen him laying there. She leaned over him to see if he was alive. That's when Brother Bashir slid a long side of the wall and back through the house to make his escape.

She never seen him. All he heard was her screaming for help and crying.

The end.

www.ingramcontent.com/pod-product-compliance
Lightning Source LLC
Chambersburg PA
CBHW060644260626
47161CB00008B/2990